CLEAN SWEEP

WAR OF THE SUBMARINE

R.G. ROBERTS

Contents

Chapter One

One Last Shot

29 September 2039, in route from the Strait of Malacca to Perth, Australia

World War III three had been kind to John Dalton. Oh, not at first. He started the war on an admiral's staff, in the kind of job that supposedly made an ambitious officer's career. Then they got an aircraft carrier shot out from under them after that admiral started the war, which shot a giant, gaping hole in any expectations or hopes for the future John had. After that, he thought he'd be stuck on that miserable staff for the rest of the war, but a twist of fate—plus one supposedly up-and-coming captain freezing up under pressure—brought him to USS *Razorback*, where he'd done pretty well for himself.

More than well, particularly during that last battle. John didn't believe in counting kills before he wrote his patrol report, but if his XO was right, *Razorback* had just smashed the American record for most enemy warships sunk in one patrol.

Come to think of it, he really should get to writing that patrol report. They were a day out of the Strait of Malacca, and it was overdue. But John had always sucked at administrative crap.

His eyes drifted to the calendar over his desk. His least favorite admiral was running for the Senate next month. Heaven help him, John was afraid McNally would get in. But that wasn't John's problem. The war of the submarine was.

That was a problem John could deal with. Much better than some of his friends, sadly. Charlie Buchanan, his old Academy classmate, had ridden *New Hampshire* to the bottom. Ken Partridge, a former shipmate, went down in *Delaware*; he'd gotten half his crew off, but the last anyone saw of Ken, he'd been trying to save a sailor with two broken legs. Jenna Vineberg, who'd been John's own XO when he commanded *Cero,* sank two frigates before a third got her and *Drum* with depth charges. The list went on, friends and acquaintances, along with a few people he outright hated. All of them with boats sunk or dead, but usually both.

As for John, he was America's top submariner. For the moment. He knew how fleeting that crown was. Commander Kurt Kins had worn it for a few months before *Darter* went down with all hands. John didn't much miss Kins as a person; he was a reckless practical joker with no sense of timing or decency, but he'd been a damned good tactician, and his loss hurt the navy. So did the loss of a *Cero*-class submarine and her trained crew.

Groaning, John sat up in bed and kicked his blankets off. One of the best things about being the captain was having his own private cabin. It was small but nice, and the mattress on *Razorback* was almost brand-new. Commanding a two-year-old attack submarine was apparently good for his back.

But not for his bladder. He'd drunk too much coffee to stay awake during the Third Battle of the SOM, and while going to sleep had been easy, his innards wouldn't let him stay that way. Maybe after he got rid of a pot or two of digested coffee, he could go back to sleep. It beat lurking around control and pretending this wasn't his very last underway on *Razorback*.

Finished in the cabin's attached bathroom, John tried not to look in the mirror. He looked like death warmed up in the microwave, he was sure. It was the middle of the night by *Razorback's* clock, and his boat vibrated gently as she sprinted and drifted south toward Australia. No captain in his right mind would be awake right now. Aging men with too-small bladders need not apply.

Defeated, John sat down at his computer and pulled up the email that would bring his second command tour to a screeching halt.

John,

I know I promised you some time off before your next command—and another go 'round with your boat—but I need your ass back in Perth. It turns out that Captain Shapiro is pregnant with triplets. Needless to say, we need to get her ass off of Nereus as fast as possible. No one wants the risk of having a pregnant captain going to war—even an old dinosaur like me.

Get your ass and your boat back as fast as you can and prepare for a change of command. Your crew will get some time off while I juggle people and get them a new CO sooner than intended.

Well done in the SOM. Good hunting on the way home.

Marco

Reading it for the fifth time filled him with a mixture of trepidation and joy. On one hand, it was damned nice to be recognized as capable and *desirable*—in a professional way—by the commander of all submarines in the Pacific and Indian Oceans. Vice Admiral Marco Rodriquez, known affectionately as "Uncle Marco" in the fleet, didn't suffer fools at all, and he sure as hell didn't handpick anyone for command that wasn't capable. Knowing he'd been singled out to advance his career made him flush with pleasure.

Still, he'd hoped for a little more time. Rubbing his eyes, John stared at the screen and wished for another month. Maybe two. But damn, triplets weren't going to wait, and no one wanted a pregnant mom underway during wartime. That was just a stupid risk to take, and Uncle Marco wasn't an idiot.

The second email from COMSUBPAC, however, had been less expected. Yet it made John grin from ear to ear, knowing he was leaving his boat in good hands.

So, it was time for John to step up. USS *Nereus* was waiting for him, and while a submarine tender wasn't as sexy as an attack submarine, it was the next rung on his career ladder. He couldn't make admiral without—

The phone next to his desk buzzed, and John snatched it. Was he hoping for action? Hell if he knew. "Captain."

"Good morning, sir, it's the officer of the deck. Sorry to wake you, but sonar reports two bottom bounce contacts bearing one-four-three, likely military based on speed and blade count. Range approximately fifty miles. No classification yet."

"Let the XO know and I'll be up as soon as I'm out of my pajamas," John replied, wiggling his toes. One of his socks had a hole in it. Huh. How had that happened?

"Aye, sir," Lieutenant Locasta, his weapons officer, replied, and hung up.

Glancing at the second email one last time, John threw his night-clothes on the narrow bed and shrugged into a fresh set of coveralls, remembering to change out his socks for a new pair before pulling his sneakers on. He was pretty sure Uncle Marco wouldn't begrudge him another kill or two, even if it slowed *Razorback's* all-out rush toward Perth.

Heck, even if the admiral was annoyed, it wasn't like he would take John's next command away. If he'd had someone else in mind, he probably would've let John keep *Razorback* for at least the year he'd been promised. Ten months—ten hectic, terror- and challenge-filled months—had not been long enough.

John paused to splash water on his face before heading to the attack center. He knew his crew considered him famous for being able to pass out anywhere on the boat, so just this once, he wanted to appear fresh and awake.

They'd already caught him drooling on the wardroom table.

Twice.

Pausing in the doorway to his stateroom, John spun around and reached into a drawer to grab a small plastic bag and a blue cardboard folder. Maybe he could kill three birds with one stone today. His crew would love this.

Chapter Two

Attention to Orders

The walk to *Razorback's* attack center, known as "the conn" or sometimes just "control," was a short one from his stateroom. At zero three hundred, there weren't a lot of sailors wandering the passageways—everyone on watch was on watch, and the cooks were done with midrats and just starting to bake bread—but he paused to greet everyone he saw.

John loved leading sailors. He particularly loved this crew; it felt *wrong* to say that he had enjoyed this command ride more than he had his first command on *Cero,* but maybe it was the kind of thing one only appreciated after it was lost. He felt that keenly, now, with the clock ticking down to when he would have to hand his beautiful submarine to his successor.

Razorback was so new she'd barely had time to acquire the character special to attack submarines: a stench uniquely her own. Parts of the boat still smelled like fresh welds and new paint, though a weird combination of overcooked pizza and raw onions warred for domination down in enlisted berthing. The goat locker, or the land of the chief petty officers, contrasted that smell with one of sugar candy—probably the chief of the boat's fault—and grease. Officers Country, rather boringly, just smelled like old socks and cheese. Someday, *Razorback* would merge all those smells into something truly grotesque, at which point she would no longer be considered a new boat and would just be part of the fleet.

John had hoped to be in command when that day came, but he knew what they said about hope and military courses of action.

"How are we looking, Jimmy?" he asked Lieutenant Locasta as he walked in.

"Sonar's refined it a little now that we slowed for our scheduled drift pattern, sir," Jimmy Locasta replied. "Range looks like sixty-plus miles, likely on a parallel course to ours toward Perth."

"That's interesting." John glanced at the plot, frowning.

Perth, Australia, was the largest Grand Alliance base left in the Indian Ocean. Besides a few places like Christmas Island—which changed hands every few months—the Alliance didn't have a lot of footholds out here. Australia remained the safest port of call, a fact that probably wouldn't change even though *Razorback* helped win the Strait of Malacca back just the day before.

The Indian Ocean was a big damned place, and the Freedom Union—officially known as the Union for the Freedom and Prosperity of the Indian Ocean—had too many footholds. France, to the surprise of many, still had colonies in this part of the world. India was obviously the thousand-pound heavyweight in their own backyard, particularly given how undersea exploitation exploded their GDP in the past decade and a half. And Russia...well, Russia always wanted *more*, as evidenced by their greedy actions as the century rolled on. While France and India started the war by seizing independent and

Alliance-aligned underwater stations, Russia went for the gold and slammed the Japanese Navy into the stone age. Then they took most of Japan's stations and northernmost islands for good measure.

That left Australia and the surrounding territories as the safest place for Alliance ships and submarines to base out of, including *Razorback*.

John sighed. "Are we sure these guys aren't friends?"

"Sonar, Conn, do you have tonals on the contacts yet?" Locasta leaned into the intercom speaker to ask.

"Conn, Sonar, we were just about to call you. Both match straight across the board to *Gorshkov* Super Frigates, brought to you courtesy of Mother Russia."

"The Russians are getting ballsy if they've come all the way down here," another voice said.

John turned to face his XO. Lieutenant Commander Patricia Abercrombie was a tall woman, with dark skin, green eyes, and magnetism to spare. Like John, she came from a navy family, though her terrifying mother—who John had only met once—was a former surface command master chief petty officer. Her brothers were in uniform, too: one on *Gerald R. Ford,* the carrier, and another a missile tech on the boomer *Columbia*.

Pat was also the best damned XO in the navy. She could finish John's sentences and knew his tactics cold; every success he'd had was at least fifty percent due to her. They made an amazing team, and he would be sorry to leave her behind.

"I agree it's a bit frisky." He shrugged. "But it's also like they're giving us an early Christmas present by approaching like this."

"Only because we're off the normal approach to Perth, sir," she replied, gesturing at the plot. "If we were further west, like most boats, these guys would be sailing through quiet waters."

John stroked his chin, nodding. "They're not accounting for us taking the Strait of Malacca back."

"To be fair, it's been thirty-six hours." Pat shrugged. "I'm still getting used to the idea, and we were there."

Several people in control snickered. Most grinned. *Razorback* had made history in the way she blasted through the SOM like a bull in the proverbial China shop, sinking everything in her path and setting that new record for enemies sunk in a single patrol. Everyone felt good about that, particularly with a few weeks' liberty in Perth on the horizon.

"Same." John leaned over the plot to manipulate the cursor. "Looks like an intercept course puts us in range in about an hour and a half if we turn toward them at sixteen knots."

"Don't feel like turning and burning today, Captain?" Locasta asked with a grin.

John chuckled. "I think we stressed the reactor enough yesterday." He glanced at the clock and shook his head. "Okay, Wednesday. Whatever."

"You want to go to battle stations now, or wait a bit?" Pat asked.

"Now's smarter, in case they change course or do something dangerous." John gestured vaguely. "But let's ask Suppo to pop out some bagels or something so everyone can eat in the meantime."

"I'll give him a call."

The minutes ticked by slowly as *Razorback* went to battle stations and the cooks handed out fruit, bagels, and red "bug juice," the sort-of strawberry-flavored staple of a submariner's drinking life. John wasn't very hungry, but he tore off a bit of bagel and munched on it, anyway, watching his crew joke and smile as they got ready to face yet another enemy.

"Thirteen torpedoes left. You think that's a lucky number?" Pat asked after most people had finished their impromptu breakfast.

"It is for you." John grinned.

"Beg pardon?" She cocked her head.

"I got an email this morning. Last night?" John shrugged. "Whatever. But it means you, madam Abercrombie, are now *Commander* Patricia Abercrombie as of...about twelve hours ago, if I'm getting my time zones right."

Pat's jaw dropped. "But I'm...I'm not in zone for promotion until next year."

"As Uncle Marco would say, welcome to the consequences of your actions." John gestured her closer. "Come on over and suffer your just desserts."

"Way to go, XO!" The chief of the watch pumped an arm from the forward port corner.

Several other sailors and officers voiced agreement, grinning as Pat crossed the space to stand in front of John. That was when he reached for the folder he'd carried into control.

"Attention to orders!" he said, and everyone not manning a station snapped to attention. Promotions were one of the few times navy sailors actually stood on ceremony; otherwise, sailors were more likely to slouch and greet each other casually, like the crew was one weird, dysfunctional family that sometimes tolerated, sometimes loved, one another.

"The President of the United States, acting upon the recommendation of the Secretary of the Navy, has placed special trust and confidence in the patriotism, integrity, and abilities of Lieutenant Commander Patricia Abercrombie. In view of these special qualities and her demonstrated potential to serve in the higher grade, Lieutenant Commander Abercrombie is promoted to the permanent grade of

Commander, United States Navy, effective 30 September 2039. By order of the Secretary of the Navy."

Pat's cheeks were red, but John could see his crew grinning. "It so happens that I happen to have a few old commander ranks lying around... Does anyone have a gerber to cut off the XO's current ones?"

"I got your back, sir." Master Chief Cary Uffington stepped forward, brandishing a gerber, the favorite multi-tool of sailors navy-wide. Unfolding one of the knife tools—that version seemed to have three or four blades—Uffington carefully slid the knife under the edge of the cloth rank sewn onto Pat's coveralls.

John watched, wearing a crooked smile and holding his old metal ranks. The problem with coveralls and working uniforms—the former being the most comfortable thing in the navy wardrobe, with the latter a distant second—was that ranks, name, and specialty badges were sewn on. Oh, it made them easier to launder and nap in, but promotion ceremonies got annoying. Particularly on the rare occasion you got to surprise someone.

He supposed war was good for something, wasn't it?

Uffington freed both cloth golden oak leaves from Pat's uniform in under a minute, handing them to her so she could slip them in a pocket.

John winked. "Ready?"

"You bet, Captain."

"All right, raise your right hand." John matched actions to words, and Pat did the same. "Repeat after me."

"I, state your name—"

"I, Patricia Marie Abercrombie."

She repeated the oath after John, line by line, as the rest of the crew watched and grinned. It was the same oath every officer took, at every promotion, but somehow, the words weighed more during wartime.

I do solemnly reaffirm that I will support and defend the Constitu-
tion of the United States of America against all enemies, foreign and
domestic, and that I will continue to bear true faith and allegiance to
the Constitution and the Country whose course it directs, and that I take
this obligation freely, without any mental reservation. So help me God.

John dropped his hand and held it out for Pat to shake, which she
did, grinning from ear to ear. "Thank you, Captain," she said.

"The pleasure's all mine, Pat. It's well deserved." John smirked.
"But I'm not done with announcements just yet. Let me grab the
1MC."

Pat's eyes flicked around. "Is anyone else worried?"

"Deeply, ma'am," Lieutenant Locasta replied, his eyes dancing.

"Traitors, all of you." John waved a hand before grabbing the microphone for the boat's general announcing system. "*Razorback,* it's
the captain. I know we're on the hunt right now, but since we have
some time before the enemy obliges us with their presence, I thought
I'd make time to promote the XO. So the next time you see *Comman-*
der Abercrombie, offer her your congratulations."

He could hear a few cheers despite the closed door to control, which
made John's smile grow. Pat's proud expression warmed his heart even
more, too; damn, he was proud of her. Pat had been a consummate
professional when John came on board, but he liked to think he'd
shined up her tactical skills even more.

"But there's one last thing. I know you've all been wondering what
happens when we get to Perth. My change of command is on the
horizon, much sooner than I anticipated. Leaving *Razorback* is going
to be hard, no matter how I do it...but now I know I'm leaving her in
good hands. Our mystery is solved today, ladies and gents. *Razorback's*
next commanding officer will be no one other than our very own
Commander Patricia Abercrombie."

"*What?*" Pat's jaw dropped as Master Chief Uffington slapped her on the shoulder so hard she staggered.

John just met her eyes, still speaking to the crew. "Now I know that I will be leaving *Razorback* in the best of hands."

"Captain..." Pat's voice was a whisper, almost impossible to hear over the crew's celebrations. "I know I passed my command qual, but I hadn't dared hope..."

"You've been with *Razorback* since the very beginning," John replied, hanging up the microphone. "Who could possibly be better?"

"Thank you." Her smile was watery, but John couldn't blame her. He'd probably get all weepy when he had to make his change of command speech, even if handing his boat over to Pat was the best possible scenario. "Did you make this happen?"

He laughed. "I don't have the power. Uncle Marco does what he wants to. We were just lucky that it went our direction this time."

"Then I guess I should—"

"Conn, Sonar, active sonar emissions, bearing zero-four-one!" a voice from the speaker in the center of control cut her off. "Range medium, hard to determine, sounds like dipping sonar."

"Son of a gun." John shook his head, feeling stupidity curling around his bones.

"Sounds like one of those Russian destroyers has a helo sanitizing their path." Pat made a face. "And we walked right into it."

"Well, let's run right out of it. Time to drop the stealth and get them before they get us." Inspiration struck John. "Why don't you take the conn?"

"Me? What?" Pat cocked her head, narrowing her eyes like he was speaking Swahili. "You're still the captain."

"For another couple of days. Consider this the P-CO check ride you're not going to get." John grinned.

"Sir, if that helo has a torpedo on board—"

"Evade it." John figured the helicopter couldn't shoot from their range, or they'd have done it already, but Pat had a good point. Being reckless had already gotten plenty of their compatriots killed in the war. "Then sink the destroyers and the helicopter will bug out for the nearest land mass it can find. It won't have fuel to play around with sinking us."

"I think you've gone a little crazy," she said.

"Maybe it's the thought of going to a surface ship driving me mad." John made a face. "You know how those skimmers are. I'm going to have to hang out with them all the time."

Pat shot him a long-suffering look. "You're not going to go take a nap or something if I do this, are you?"

"No, I'll be right beside you." John had every confidence in Pat, but *Razorback* was still his boat until he signed her over. That meant she was his responsibility until the bitter end, and in the unlikely occurrence that Pat *did* freeze up...John would be there to take the reins.

Besides, it was better to know now if she couldn't hack it. John thought she could, but the pressure of being the captain was higher than being the XO. That was the genius behind prospective commanding officer, or P-CO check rides. It gave an experienced captain the chance to see the *potential* captain in action...and it gave a new CO a shoulder to lean on if they needed one.

Command was lonely. John knew that better than most, having now succeeded captaining two attack subs, one in war and one at peace. Command at *war* broke a lot of people; responsibility for all those other lives and having the power to kill so many more was both a terrifying and heady feeling. Not everyone was suited to command,

and that was all right—as long as they didn't drag others to the bottom with them.

Chapter Three

First Shot

P at squared her shoulders. "This is the XO. I have the conn."

"The XO has the conn," Locasta replied.

"Sonar, Conn, bearing to Russian destroyers?" Pat asked.

"Conn, Sonar, zero-seven-six and zero-seven-nine."

"Conn, aye. Left standard rudder, all ahead flank for forty knots." Pat glanced at John. "You think any faster is a risk with that helo up there?"

"I think we've already shot off our missiles, so the only option is to get in close and fast." He shrugged. "Trying to lose a helo takes all day. I think turning and burning in is the right choice."

"The only good thing about dipping sonar is that it can only be in one place at a time." Pat's smile turned grim. "So if we get out of its range, the helo's going to have to pull it in and reset."

"By which point you'll have wiggled onto a different heading and they might not find us again." John smiled. "Good thinking."

John did some quick mental math. *Razorback* speeding up to forty knots meant the rate of closure with the destroyers was fifty-six knots. At their range, that decreased the intercept time to right around an hour. Not bad, particularly if Pat could lose the helicopter hunting them.

His XO—soon to be his relief—*did* have a good tactical mind. In fact, John was pretty sure Pat was sneakier and less conventional than he was. She reminded him of Alex Coleman sometimes. Wouldn't those two have made a great pair? In a just world, Alex would've gotten a boat like *Razorback* instead of getting saddled with *Jimmy Carter*. Having Dick O'Kane's famous cribbage set on board didn't make up for *Jimmy Carter's* advanced age or the fact that she was six inches from being turned into razor blades.

John was old enough to remember when *Jimmy Carter* had been *the* plum command in the attack sub community. He'd tried really hard to get orders to the boat as a department head, but the timing didn't work out, and he ended up on *John Warner*, instead. Things worked out in the end, and he met one of the best friends he'd ever have, but it still sucked now that the same best friend had been screwed over by big navy and sent to the land of the dead on *Jimmy Carter*. Particularly since he had George Kirkland with him.

Kirkland had been navigator on *Razorback* before Locasta, and sailors still told stories about Kirkland's micromanaging ineptitude. Jimmy Locasta was popular solely on the basis of *not being Kirkland*, though his competence and good humor also won the crew over.

Shaking himself, John refocused on the situation at hand while Pat drove *Razorback* in for the kill. Her best tactic was the one they already discussed: corkscrewing around their base course to force the helicopter to lose track every time it pulled its dipping sonar out of the water to change position. Obviously, the helicopter was communicating with both destroyers, because once *Razorback* entered RGB-60 range, the destroyers started launching rocket-propelled depth charges at where they *thought* the enemy submarine was.

Neither destroyer slowed, however. Were they eager for a kill? Judging from the amount of ordnance they were happy to throw into the water, John thought they were.

"Nice job," he said quietly. "You keep chasing salvos, and we just might kill them before they even get a piece of us."

"That's the idea." Pat flashed him a smile. "I was reading some World War II patrol reports, and it seems like what they did with gunfire works with depth charges, too."

"Never occurred to me, but I like it." John scratched his chin. "Remind me to write this one up and give you credit."

"Better coming from you, sir. The egomaniacs might listen. You're on your way to the top, and everyone knows it."

"By which you mean I've topped out. I'm done after this." John leaned against the chart table and crossed his arms. "This is your show from here on out, Pat."

Forty-five minutes later, their luck ran out. Or maybe the Russians' luck came in. John would never figure that out, but it didn't really matter when a lucky shot of depth charges soared across the expanse between the enemy destroyers and *Razorback*...and bracketed the submarine.

Razorback shuddered and shimmied, her lights flickering as pipes burst and water sprayed. Sailors leaped to repair the damage even as they staggered and struggled for balance. John shook his head as his ears rung, trying to clear out the fog and concentrate. To his right, Pat picked herself up off the deck.

"Weps, do you have a firing solution?" she asked.

"Yes, ma'am. Longer range than preferred, still fifteen thousand yards."

"Damn." She glanced at John. "It's still too risky to shoot from this far out, isn't it?"

"Honestly, I'm not sure. We've been getting in close out of habit, but now that we have the new torpedoes…" He gestured vaguely. "The game might be different against surface ships."

Pat chewed her lip, and John could almost read her mind. The U.S. Navy had started the war with the Mark 48 CBASS torpedo, their old, reliable friend. Unfortunately, the CBASS was slower than the torpedoes their enemy fielded; while it had a bigger warhead, it still had to *hit* the enemy to kill them, and it often couldn't do that…unless a sub got into spitting distance before firing.

The Mark 84 ASV, or Advanced Spearfish Variant, however, was a different story. A joint American-British effort, the ASV was slightly longer ranged and thirty-three knots faster than its older sister. John had continued to get in close to kill the enemy; he didn't like giving anyone a chance to run away when he could use *Razorback's* stealth to creep up on them. But when the enemy already knew you were there…

"Make tubes one through four ready in all respects, including opening the outer doors," Pat ordered.

"Make tubes one through four ready in all respects, including opening the outer doors, aye, ma'am!"

"Conn, Sonar, splashes to starboard," Sonar reported. "Likely bearing zero-three-four. Detection is difficult with the noise topside and our speed."

"Conn, aye. Right standard rudder." Pat turned *Razorback* to chase these splashes as well. Had the destroyer figured her tactic out? Unlikely. They were still moving fast, and if *Razorback's* sonar picture was murky, it was far worse on the destroyers.

Modern technology claimed to be able to filter out own ship's speed and self-noise out, but John always found that lacking. It was particularly bad on surface ships, whose sonar wasn't as deep *in* the water as a submarine's was. Active sonar was a surface ship's best weapon, and—

"Conn, Sonar, active sonar! Destroyer number one, track seven-zero-nine-three, has gone active!"

"Firing point procedures, tubes one and three, track seven-zero-nine-three!" Pat snapped.

It didn't take long. *Razorback's* crew was sharp, well-trained, and fresh off a victory in the Strait of Malacca where they sank eight enemy warships.

"Solution ready!"

"Ship ready!"

"Fire!" Pat wasted no time. "Weps, set tubes two and four up on the other destroyer."

"On it, ma'am!"

John just smiled as he watched his crew at work. The feeling was bittersweet; they weren't going to be his for much longer, but *damn* was he proud of them. He'd been fortunate to lead them for thirteen months, hadn't he? The alternative was driving a desk or following Admiral McNally into his political ambitions. Yuck.

It wasn't that John blamed McNally for being ambitious. *John* was ambitious. He wanted to get at least three stars, preferably four. His dream of dreams was to become the chief of naval operations one day and to run the whole dang show. But McNally's ambition was allied to carelessness and stupidity. He'd panicked, sunk the wrong nation's submarine, and started a war that he then tried to sit out by shutting down and leaving John and Captain Julia Rosario to handle things.

A couple thousand American sailors died that day, all because Jeff McNally couldn't wrap common sense and tactical aptitude around his ambition. John was well rid of him.

"Tubes two and four, fire!" Pat's order brought John back to the present.

"Tubes two and four fired electrically. Two fish running hot, straight, and normal," Sonar reported.

"Very well." Pat glanced at John. "Why do torpedoes seem to go slower when you're the one who shoots them?"

He chuckled. "Perception is reality."

"Torps one and three in final acquisition. Both have terminal homing," a watchstander said.

"Very well." Pat wiped her hands off on the legs of her coveralls.

"Conn, Sonar, destroyers are maneuvering. Screw noise increasing. I think they're turning into a torpedo evasion maneuver." A pause. "Dipping sonar close aboard. I think the helo has us cold."

"Time to clear datum, Pat," John said in an undertone.

Her head jerked up, eyes wide. "What? Oh, shit." Pat shook herself. "Weps, cut the wires and close the outer doors. We'll have to trust the ASVs are smart enough to hit surface ships on their own."

"Weps, aye," Locasta replied.

Cutting the wires was a risk; it took away *Razorback's* real time control of the torpedoes. However, remaining connected to them kept *Razorback* from maneuvering the way she needed to if she was going to get clear of whatever retribution the destroyers launched.

"Conn, Sonar, splashes! Splashes directly overhead!"

"All ahead flank!" Pat barked. "Dive, make your depth eight hundred feet."

John nodded, keeping his hands in his pockets and resisting the urge to interfere. Was this how flag officers felt? He didn't like it, but he supposed he could get used to it. Better he learn now, when there was no one but *Razorback's* crew to notice if he made a fool of himself. At least they knew and respected him. He let out a slow breath. Pat had done the right thing, diving under the layer and sprinting away as fast as she could. But everything depended on what depth those charges had been programmed to explode at, didn't it?

Razorback trembled lightly as she picked up speed, racing for deeper water. John carefully kept his face blank; he wasn't sure if this was the tactic he would've chosen, but that didn't make it *wrong*.

He'd just watched too many VDR recordings of subs that went down following standard American tactics to run for deep water when enemy weapons came their way. And once you were deep, the odds of any escape decreased with every foot of pressure...

Boom!

The first explosion came from astern and well above them. *Razorback* shuddered again, rattling and rolling with the blow. The second was further away, and the shockwave barely caught her spinning propulsor, but the third was closer. Close enough to feel the concussion through the hull, which took the blow like a champ but jumped *up* in the water by a few feet, making sailors and gear roll toward the bow.

The stack of uneaten bagels took the worst of it, taking flight and plastering themselves against the forwardmost bulkhead. Cream cheese decorated the depth indicator before it dribbled off, seeping onto the deckplates.

Master Chief Uffington swore, picked his ballcap up off the floor, and then helped the sailor at the helm re-fasten her seatbelt so she stopped flying out of her chair.

"Hope everyone secured for sea." Uffington grinned.

"If they didn't do that before we left, they deserve to have broken gear." John glanced sadly at the bagels. He should've eaten one earlier, but he forgot in all the excitement of promoting Pat.

"Maybe next time we get the bagels *after* the action, Captain," Uffington said, his voice mild.

"Talk to the XO. She's the one who's going to make the next messy decision like that." John grinned to hide the pang in his stomach. Damn, he was going to miss this boat.

"Conn, Sonar, explosions on both bearings! It looks like we got both of them!"

Someone cheered; Pat's grin was huge enough to power the sun. "Well done, everyone," she said. "Now—"

Boom.

"Shit, did one of them get a last launch off?" Pat asked as *Razorback* buckled and the lights went off and then on again. Battle lanterns flicked on, then off, and then on again, bathing control in eerie yellow light.

"Sounds like." John licked his lips, counting seconds and struggling to hold the recommendation back. If Pat was smart...

"Hard left rudder. OOD, let's get the hell out of here," Pat said. "No reason to hang around where the rest of that salvo might cook us."

"Yes, ma'am!"

Chapter Four

Icons

The rest of their transit to Perth was quiet. John spent several hours with Pat, going over the necessary turnover items. Fortunately, with her as the XO, the list was remarkably short. It wasn't like he needed to tell her about their personnel problems; Pat was more in tune with most of those than he was. She knew about Jimmy Locasta's affair with the mayor of Perth. Both parties were married, and neither knew the navy was aware of their trysts, but until the relationship became detrimental to good order and discipline, John didn't see a reason to act. Jimmy was a great officer, and what he did in his off time was his business.

Master Chief Uffington was the problem John felt guilty leaving in Pat's hands. Uffington had tried to retire three times, only for the navy to tell him a resounding no, because there was a critical shortage of qualified COBs. He'd stopped trying in John's third month on board, but now he was threatening to drop his papers again. Not, thankfully, because of the upcoming change of command—in fact, John hoped that might make him stay—but because he was old, tired, and *Razorback* had already broken the record for most enemies sunk in a single patrol.

Would they add the two destroyers to John's total for his last patrol, or would they count as Pat's first? If John had his way, it'd be the latter. He already owned the record. Why pad it?

Finally, his boat surfaced one last time near Beacon Head, right on schedule. John liked to be on schedule, and Pat always facilitated that. He hoped her incoming XO, whoever it was, would be half as competent and organized as Pat.

"Let's put a broomstick up," John said as *Razorback* entered the channel leading toward Naval Station Perth.

Pat twisted to stare at him. "For a clean sweep?"

"We killed everything we shot at, didn't we?" John grinned. "I know it's not peacetime, where we're on our way back from sea trials, or we shot tomahawks at someone...but it'd be nice to use one for its original purpose, wouldn't it?"

"I like that." Pat turned to one of the quartermasters. "Charlie, go find a broomstick, will you?"

"You got it, ma'am." Charlie grinned and vanished.

According to legend, the tradition of using a broom for a clean sweep was older than the U.S. Navy, having started in battle between the Dutch and the British in the late seventeenth century. However, the tradition for American warships started in World War II.

Like many submarine traditions, it started on the first USS *Wahoo* (SS 238), commanded by the legendary Mush Morton. On Morton's first patrol in command, *Wahoo* sunk every enemy ship she encountered and then returned to port with a broom tied to her mast. From there, the tradition was born, and submarines throughout the war continued in *Wahoo's* footsteps.

John's heart fluttered as he watched Charlie bring the broom up to the grinning lookouts along with a small bundle of line. Laughing, the lookouts tied it to the radar mast before looking down.

"Good enough, Captain?" one asked.

"Perfect," John replied. He glanced at Pat, whose smile mirrored his own. "Never thought I'd make myself feel just a little like Mush Morton."

She coughed on a laugh. "Does that make me Dick O'Kane, sir?" she asked, referring to Morton's equally legendary XO—who went on to be the most successful single commander in the Second World War.

"I've always idolized O'Kane myself," John admitted. "More measured, less manic."

"I don't know. It was Morton who shook up the sub service and made us look at our tactics and realize we sucked," she replied. "You've done that a bit. I don't think the comparison's that bad."

John gulped. "No, thank you. I don't go around offering to wrestle people, and I'm sure not someone with the nickname 'Mushmouth.' That man was a menace. A useful one, but I prefer O'Kane's measured tactics to the down-the-throat shots Morton was known for."

"They do fit modern warfare better, that's for sure." She glanced at the broom. "You think anyone's going to be mad about that?"

"Let 'em die mad. You can blame me if anyone shits a brick."

***

1 October 2039, Perth, Australia

He should have guessed that Admiral Rodriquez would meet them on the pier.

"Well done, son." Marco pumped John's hand with more enthusiasm than was necessary; would it sprain his wrist? Only time would tell. "And two more destroyers on the way home? Makes for a *damned* fine patrol."

"I turned the boat over to the XO for a mini check ride on those two," John replied. "Pat did fantastic. Those should be her kills, not mine."

Two eyebrows shot straight up in Marco Rodriquez's tanned face. "Your boat, your call. You ready for a change of command?"

"Today?" John gulped and then remembered to close his mouth so he didn't look like a blowfish.

"Nah, I figured I'd give you three days to get your shit sorted and a speech written. Your wife's flying in, by the way. Got her a nice VIP room at the best hotel in town, so you two can have a little leave before you take over *Nereus* on the eleventh."

John blinked. "Janet's coming?" He'd hoped she could come out, but last they'd talked, all the military flights out to Perth were full, with no hope of a civilian squeezing on board.

"You bet she is. You've done good for the navy, John. It's time the navy gave you something back." Rodriquez squinted. "Is that a fucking broom I see?"

John rocked back on his heels, feeling like he had whiplash. "Yes, sir, it is. Felt appropriate, all things considered."

"Fuck me with a rusty spoon, why didn't I think of that?" Rodriquez shook his head. "Good thinking, even if it shows what a numb-nuts admiral I've become. Clean sweep. You get everything you shot at?"

"We did." John shrugged. "Of course, we couldn't sink the helicopter one of the Russian destroyers launched, but I don't think it had enough fuel to land anywhere, so it probably crashed. Can we call that a kill for Pat, too?"

Rodriquez snorted. "Don't push it, kid."

John chuckled. "I'd never dream of it, Admiral." He hesitated. "Do I really get a whole week between the ceremonies?"

"You think I'd wring you that dry?" Rodriquez shook his head. "There might be a war on, John, but I know you and your crew busted ass in the SOM. Get through your change of command here—and I've got people setting up all the ruffles and flourishes, so don't worry about that shit—and then you and *Razorback's* peeps all get some much-deserved R&R. You'll have to turn over with Shapiro during that week, but it's not ready to pop for another five months, so you'll have her full attention."

"I...I really appreciate the leave, sir. I probably need a reset, particularly after the SOM."

"I'm just glad this trip through there was better than your first," Rodriquez said quietly. "I remember how beat to shit you looked when we first met."

"I, well, I wasn't at my best."

"None of us were that day, John." Rodriquez slapped him on the shoulder. "Now, go settle what you need to here. Hang out with your officers. Do your hail and farewell. If they've got any fucking sense at all, they'll miss you like hell."

"They've got Pat. They're going to be in the best hands." John glanced back at *Razorback,* not liking the thought of giving her up in three days. "Thank you for that, sir. I owe you one."

"If she's half as good as you, Dalton, you don't owe me jack."

"She might be better." John smiled sadly. "She's definitely more creative." He took a deep breath. "I know you're looking for a Mush Morton, Admiral. That's not me. I'm too conservative at heart. But Pat might fit the bill."

"You're already thinking like an admiral, aren't you?" Rodriquez cocked his head. "Don't die on *Nereus.* We've got plans for you."

"As long as they're not casting me as Mush Morton, I'm game."

"Nah, I'll keep looking."

Chapter Five

Poor Decisions

4 October 2039

Navies loved traditions. While submariners might've been considered the *weird* children in a lot of navies, they were no different on that front. That meant any arriving or departing officer was celebrated at a "Hail and Farewell," where the officers got together, ate, drank, and generally made merry—and stupid—at one another's expense.

John endured the roasting with good humor. Ensign Nelson did a surprisingly good impression of him, a fact he learned when the junior officers did a silly skit revolving around John falling asleep in the wardroom and no one being able to find him when an enemy was approaching. It was hammed up for laughs, but John didn't mind—even with Janet beside him, watching his crew mock him.

After all, Janet was a child of Norwich University, a place *far* more brutal when it came to mocking their own than John had ever dreamed of. She laughed harder than anyone else.

Did John get drunk? A little. He had both his speeches done for *both* changes of command—usually people didn't have two of them within eight days—and that meant he was free to be stupid. At least a little.

But he made sure not to be too hungover when it came time to give *Razorback* to Pat. He wanted to remember every moment, and not with a blazing headache.

"Are you ready?" Janet asked, fastening the collar of his summer dress white uniform.

It still felt odd to wear his summer uniform in October, but Australia was an entirely different hemisphere than John was used to being stationed in. So he wore what the navy called his "choker whites" for ceremonies, complete with the pearly white shoes that were easier to get dirty than a white dress on a toddler.

"The look on your face says you think I'm not," he replied.

Janet snorted. "I know you. You got drunk and almost missed your change of command on *Cero*. I had to drag you out of bed."

"Hey, I got up with the alarm."

"After snoozing it three times."

John shrugged, feeling his rack of medals shift. Wow, it was still weird to see a Navy Cross there—with another to come, if Uncle Marco got his way. Wild. "I'm awake and coherent. And only mildly hung over."

She patted his shoulder. Janet was a tall woman, right up there with Nancy Coleman in terms of height. But they were physical opposites in every other way; Janet was blond, with sparkling green eyes and a wicked sense of humor. Nancy, like John, was a straight and narrow type, but her old college roommate had always been the one to drag her into trouble.

John didn't mind trouble. He just liked it to be of the type that shot back during wartime. Anything else was boring.

"You're bad at letting go," she replied.

"I'm trying a new tactic. I put Pat in command for the last few days so I could get used to it." John squirmed. "It...sort of worked."

"Does going to another ship help?"

"Not really." He grimaced. "My last surface ship experience was...bad."

"You mean McNally's staff." Janet's voice went flat.

"And the battle that came out of his stupidity, yes." John swallowed hard and tried to distract himself by ensuring his ceremonial officer's sword hung correctly at his left side. "The last time I was on a surface ship, it was being rescued off the one that sank out from under me. Not a great track record."

"At least you won't be under McNally this time?" She squeezed his hand.

"No, he's running for Senate, and polls say he'll get in."

"Bastard. I wish I could vote for his opponent, but we don't live in Georgia." Janet scowled. "Neither does he, from what I know. He's just doing one of those 'I have a house for tax purposes' things that so many of the rat bastards do."

"I wish I was surprised." John shook himself. "Let's not talk about him now. He's likely to ruin the day."

"All right. How about this? You go out there, knock your speech out of the park, and *I'll* rescue you from the reporters afterward, and we'll go out to a great place I found for dinner, just the two of us."

"Sounds like a deal." John wasn't going to pass up time alone with his wife, not after only talking to her on phone calls and video chats for the last thirteen months. And, well, if he had to make a speech to do it and give up his submarine...John didn't mind speeches, and he didn't have a choice on the last part.

It was time to bite the bullet and move on with his life.

***

11 October 2039

"John."

Hands shook him, but John Dalton was deep in a dream about a talking coffee mug, aliens, and potato chips with legs. Mumbling something unintelligible, he tried to roll over, only for those same hands to shake him harder.

"John!"

The coffee mug morphed into a shark, which started chasing the deer—where had the deer come from?—and then the sky started raining potato chips. And pizza. Pizza sounded so lovely.

"John Dalton, if you don't wake up *right now*, I swear to God that I will dump an entire bucket of ice on your head and then pay the bill when the hotel objects," Janet snarled. "Make me wait and it will be *two* buckets of ice."

"Huh?" He cracked an eye open.

"That's what I thought, you idiot. Why the *hell* did you go drinking with Admiral Rodriquez last night? You knew what would happen!"

"Drinking?" John felt like his tongue was made of sandpaper. "Water?"

"Not until you sit up. Otherwise, you're getting that bucket of ice."

"You Norwich people are crazy pants."

"Guilty as charged. Now sit the hell up." She dragged him into a sitting position, and John mostly helped. His limbs felt heavy, like they were made of concrete and wanted to crumble away if he moved too fast.

He groaned, but Janet was merciless and handed him a mug of coffee. That was nice; the hotel was expensive enough to have branded coffee mugs to accompany the crappy little coffee machine.

"I'm in the big leagues now," he muttered. "Get real cups to go with the cheap, off-brand coffee."

"There's a Starbucks down the street if you're feeling human."

"No way." Squinting, John tried to put the coffee mug on the nightstand and missed on the first try. And the second. Janet saved him from a third, scowling.

"How drunk *did* you get?" she asked.

"I'm not sure I remember."

Janet sank down on the bed next to him. "John...*really?*"

"I know." Groaning again, John rubbed his eyes and wished he hadn't. It made his head ache. "I haven't been this drunk since our second anniversary."

She snorted. "No, you mean the party you went to the day *after* our anniversary."

"Hey, it was with *your* friends!" John winced. Raising his voice made his head hurt even more. "Ugh. I don't remember much, but I know Uncle Marco drank me under the table."

"I'm so sorry?"

"He's a three-star, Janet. *Old.*"

"Says the guy bucking for flag himself." She laughed and rubbed his back. "We're getting old, John."

"Don't say that."

"Too late."

With nothing left to say, John flopped back on the bed and drew a pillow over his face. Every inch of his body hurt, and the less he thought of his rolling stomach, the better. "Leave me here to die."

"Sure, I'll just go take command of that sub tender of yours. I'm sure they won't mind that I got out of the air force over ten years ago," Janet replied. "Your uniforms will look funny on me, though."

"*Nereus* will wait." John's voice was muffled under the pillow, but he didn't care. "I need sleep."

His stomach lurched like it was underway. Did it want breakfast or to vomit? John wasn't sure and decided to stay put.

How in the world had Uncle Marco drunk him under the table? John remembered a laughing challenge from the admiral—something stupid like *if you can't drink with the chiefs, you shouldn't stay in uniform*—and then tequila. Lots of tequila.

Marco Rodriquez was a hilarious son of a bitch when drunk, though. The man even did *karaoke*, which John remembered in fuzzy bits and pieces. Had Marco been singing songs from *Hamilton*? John just remembered him jumping all over the tiny stage in a drunken frenzy of music love. Then there had been something about elephants, but that was drowned by vodka.

Oh.

It wasn't breakfast his stomach wanted.

Ten minutes later, Janet wandered into the bathroom as John washed his mouth out for the fifth time.

"Your change of command is in two hours," she said. "You'd better get in the shower."

"*Two*—" John couldn't even make himself finish the sentence. He was too busy gaping like a dead blowfish.

"Shower." She pointed. "Now."

Chapter Six

Change of Command

An hour later, John was spiffed up in his choker whites, wearing every medal he owned and fighting back a pounding headache. He'd almost forgotten to put on his sword—an item he *only* wore on occasions like this—necessitating a run back to the hotel after he and Janet were five minutes down the road. Unfortunately, the gaudy thing was still there, and John strapped it around his waist without falling down.

Then he headed into the crowd in front of USS *Nereus* (AS 43), the gargantuan submarine tender that would be his. This wasn't his first time visiting the ship, of course. He hadn't spent the last week drinking, either. No, most of it was spent on *Nereus*, getting tours, meeting his future officers and crew, and going over trouble points, personnel, and maintenance with Captain Shapiro. They also did a stem-to-stern ammunition inventory, and wasn't that fun? John liked it better when he only had to account for twenty-something torpedoes and a handful of missiles.

But that was done. Most of the paperwork was signed, and he was ready to go. If only he could shake the raging monster ricocheting around in his skull. Fate, however, was not kind. The third person he ran into was Uncle Marco.

John saluted, wishing he could wear sunglasses or at least pull his cover down over his eyes to shade them. "Good morning, Admiral. I didn't know you'd be coming."

"And miss this?" Rodriquez's smile seemed normal. How was he not hung over? John felt like he'd been run over by the elephants Rodriquez babbled about when drunk. "I always ride along to make sure my manipulations work out right."

"Is that what I am? A manipulation?"

"Hey, try being the motherfucking chess master. It's headache inducing." Marco gestured vaguely. "You goddamned lot keeps calling me 'Uncle' Marco like I'm Charlie fucking Lockwood, but I'm just trying to keep everything from falling apart. And keep as many of you alive as possible."

That last sentence was delivered with a pointed look, and John swallowed as invisible needles swarmed his eyes. Damn sunlight.

"That's why I'm here, isn't it?" He took a deep breath to steady himself. Drinking had been a terrible idea. "So you can hold up the example of someone who succeeded in command and survived."

"I did tell you not to get yourself killed. Glad you listened."

John grimaced. "I'm not...I'm not sure how I feel about that."

"Don't tell me your ambition's failed you now, son. I like you better when you're shooting for stars. Makes you predictable."

"No, I still want to be an admiral." John chuckled, despite the rolling feeling in his gut. "I just—well, I'm not really sure how much I like you playing favorites with me as the favorite."

"You fucking earned it, so you'll sit down and take it." The stern glare was a far cry from the wild man singing karaoke the night before, yet somehow the mental images meshed together just fine. "We need your ass alive. You're lucky I didn't send you to the sub school to teach."

John shuddered. "Admiral, that is definitely *not* something you want me doing. Impressionable young people are...not my thing. There's a reason I don't have kids."

"I was going to send you to teach *captains*, not kids, Dalton. Don't get your panties in a twist."

"It's nice to know you're not— Oh, shit, sorry, that's the hangover talking." John shook himself before he could call a three-star admiral a dumbass. They *weren't* drinking now, so he needed to mind his tongue.

Rodriquez threw back his head, hooting with laughter. "I can see why no one trusts you around kids." He shoved John's right shoulder none too gently. "Go on. Get with the new crew and talk to Captain Shapiro before she keels over and has the triplets."

"I'm pretty sure it doesn't work like that." John hadn't been so crass as to ask *Nereus'* current captain how far along she was, but she didn't look ready to pop. At least not to him.

Rodriquez just laughed and walked away, leaving John to wander up to the woman he'd be relieving in—he checked his watch—forty-three minutes.

The crowd had grown while he chatted with the admiral; John counted a few friends, a pair of Academy classmates who ended up in the Supply Corps, and a bunch of people he didn't know. A lot of them were surface sailors. Were they former *Nereus* hands? He wasn't sure.

Captain Andrea Shapiro was, like John, a submariner. It was one of the requirements for commanding a submarine tender whose entire job it was to take care of submarines. Driving a ship on the surface was different, sure, but giving TLC to a hotdog stuck to a nuclear power plant was a lot more complicated than learning to drive a surface ship.

Or at least John sure hoped so. He hadn't gotten a chance to get underway with his future command, and he hadn't gotten any simulator time, either. Aside from driving *Enterprise* a bit on a whim when he'd thought he wanted to earn his surface officer of the deck qualification, John hadn't driven a surface ship since he was a midshipman.

Nereus hung over the red-white-and-blue-draped podium like an ominous mountain of navy gray metal. Damn, she was big. Almost as tall as that ill-fated *Enterprise* had been. There would be another one soon, though, wouldn't there? John had heard that the weird aviation side of the navy had convinced SecNav to name yet *another* carrier *Enterprise* before the old one was barely settled on the bottom of the SOM. He wasn't sure how he felt about that.

Swallowing, he forced his mind away from the last surface ship he served on. *Nereus* wasn't likely to face a missile storm. No, her main threat was enemy submarines...and her best defense was the friendly submarines she was built to repair and rearm.

John hoped he'd made a few friends along the way to watch his underside. Lord knew he'd need them.

"Hanging in there, Andrea?" he asked, stepping up on the raised platform.

Andrea Shapiro was a short, dark-skinned woman with a narrow face and hawk-like eyes. John remembered her from the Academy, where she'd been a senior when he was a lowly plebe. Back then, she was a battalion commander and he was lower than dirt, but those green eyes still missed nothing. Now, however, they were equals in rank, and she smiled to see him.

"My back is killing me and my shoes feel like they're two sizes two small," she replied. "How's the hangover?"

"Do I look that bad?" John stifled a yawn.

"Word's going around base about Uncle Marco's wild party and how you got him to sing karaoke." She snickered. "I wish these three would let me stay up past nine. I was out like a light."

"I didn't dare him." He scrunched up his nose, thinking. "I'm pretty sure that was one of the chiefs. There were two there from his first boat."

"That'll do it." She laughed. "Still, you should take credit. The crew's half submariners. It'll build you a legend."

"I think I'm all right," John replied, glancing into the crowd to see Janet chatting with Pat, who looked both proud and still a little shocked to be wearing a commander's stripes.

Too bad his parents couldn't be here, but at least they were watching virtually. Both were retired flag officers, which meant high-powered government or quasi-government jobs, even in retirement. His mother worked for the secretary of defense—fortunately, on the aviation side of things, otherwise John would've represented a submarine-sized conflict of interest—and his father worked for a strategic think tank in Washington, D.C. He'd talked to both at length before he started drinking and knew they were proud of him, but it wasn't the same as having them there.

He wished his closest friends, like Alex and Nancy, could be here, but both were still underway. So was Gunnar Pavolko, commanding the ballistic missile submarine *Challenger*. At least he knew where Alex and Nancy were. Gunnar was out somewhere, lurking in the ocean in case the world was stupid enough to take this war nuclear.

Thankfully, even being at war with three nuclear powers didn't make John think India, Russia, or France was stupid enough to start lobbing nuclear weapons around.

Once you started that, you could never go back.

Janet caught his eye and winked, so John forced his mind off of strategic matters and back to the change of command. He would've invited newer friends, like Admiral Julia Rosario, who'd saved his ass in the First Battle of the SOM, but Julia's flagship was underway with Nancy. So she was right out. So was Admiral Larkin, who was in command of a carrier strike group sailing off America's East Coast. Aaron Larkin had been John's captain during his own XO tour, and he was still a mentor figure for him.

Still, a good chunk of his *Razorback* crew—now Pat's, but forever a part of John's history—was here to see him take charge of his new command, weren't they? That made his chest grow warm. They were on leave and could be out having fun, but instead, several dozen of his former sailors chose to put on their dress whites and stand in the sun.

Shapiro chuckled. "Yeah, you'll do fine. You're everyone's fair-haired boy these days."

"What makes you say that?" John twisted to face her again.

"You're the man of the moment. Broke Kurt Kins's record for most enemies killed in one patrol *and* lived to tell the tale. Part of me is surprised that Uncle Marco dared pull you out of a boat."

John's smile was crooked. "There was a lecture about not dying in there. He seems to think we have an expiration date."

"I'm not sure he's wrong." Her eyes drifted to the middle distance, staring at something John couldn't see. "We pick up a lot more survivors than we repair battle-damaged subs, John. Have you dredged anyone out of the water yet?"

"I can't say I have."

"Whichever side they're from, it's not pleasant." She grimaced. "No one escapes a sinking submarine without losing someone or something. They've all been dark places."

"I can't say I enjoyed the swim after *Enterprise* went down, but I was blown free." John swallowed, his voice dropping to a ragged whisper. A submariner didn't need much imagination to picture a concussive blast and water rushing in as the lights vanished, leaving you in a dark tube with a hundred of your closest friends. "Not quite the same."

"No, I don't think so."

He shook himself. "This is a lovely conversation to have today. I should ask you about your future. You going home?"

"Yeah, the navy says they want me Stateside. Something about high-risk pregnancies, war, and my husband threatening murder. Not necessarily in that order." She smiled again. "He says he'll knock me out and drag me on a plane if he has to."

"That's, uh, ominous."

"Not as bad as you think. He's a neurologist. Good with chemicals, and has a medical degree to prove it."

"Well, then I bet you'll be glad for a break." John hadn't thought of what he'd do with one since he'd rushed into the war. *Nereus* was so much lower key than *Razorback* that it had to be like a vacation, right?

Shapiro shrugged. "My first command tour wasn't nearly as hectic as the one you just finished. I got off *Alaska* before the war started."

Had she shot at anyone? Had *anyone* on *Nereus*? John thought it was impolite to ask her on her way out, but he'd have to talk to the XO later. He didn't intend to run around with his new—and meager—guns blazing, but it was good to know if they worked.

After all, he was well aware of what the navy called "preventative maintenance." The navy loved taking apart perfectly working pumps to *check if they worked right* and then putting them back together again...with the inevitable result being that the pump didn't work as well as it did before a sailor started fiddling.

Yeah. Wartime had killed a lot of bad habits, but that one still lingered. John reminded himself to check on the beans, bullets, and Band-Aids. That was the best way to keep his ship and new crew safe.

"Looks like it's time," Shapiro said when he didn't reply, gesturing to where her—soon to be his—XO had stepped up to the speaker's podium.

John grimaced. Pity he couldn't take any more pills for his headache. There were going to be a *lot* of speeches today. There always were at change-of-command ceremonies. The unfortunate part was that he had to go last, which meant he had to stay awake through all of them. His new crew also needed to see him looking professional, not like some bum drooling and asleep with his head on a table. They'd see that side of him soon enough!

He didn't normally mind speeches. They were just part of the game, the price of moving up in the navy. But with a herd of buffalo tromping around inside his skull... Nah, John was sure he'd be fine. He'd faced enemy ships and submarines at war. How much worse could a speech be?

Steeling himself, John cocked his head and daydreamed of water-skiing through a boring speech by Ms. Bowing, the christening sponsor of *Nereus*, who had for some insane reason flown all the way out to Australia *during a war* to talk about her late husband's naval career. Normally, John would feign interest or actually find something intriguing in the speech itself, but today his hungover brain just couldn't get past a civilian getting on a plane to talk for fifteen minutes—five past her time limit—during a war.

He hoped she had family out here or something; otherwise it was a remarkably stupid move. Was that a bad omen?

Admiral Rodriquez was much more entertaining. He skipped the "honor and glory of service" crap and went straight to highlighting Andrea Shapiro's career and time on *Nereus* before talking John up enough to make a comedian blush. His jokes were cleaner than usual, however, and John wondered if three-star admirals rated speech writers. COMSUBPAC probably did, didn't he? Either way, the speech was funny and made the crowd laugh. Captain Shapiro was next, and she was boring by comparison, though as a submariner, Andrea probably expected that. She focused on thanking her crew and her family and didn't put too fine a point on how her pregnancy forced her to leave the ship early.

Then it was John's turn.

Standing, he straightened his uniform and strode to the podium. The Australian sun was bright in his eyes, but at least he could look down at his notes for some of the speech to hide from it. John usually preferred to memorize speeches, but he hadn't had much time with this one. Writing it between engagements on *Razorback* might not have been the best idea, but it had been all he had.

Then he got to the lectern, patted his pocket, and realized he'd left the stupid speech in his hotel room, right next to Janet's extra purse.

So much for notes. He'd have to rely on his memory, after all.

"Ladies and gentlemen, Admiral Rodriquez, Captain Shapiro, *Nereus* sailors, friends and family, thank you for having me today. I know I'm an unfamiliar face"—a few sailors snickered, given how John had toured *Nereus* no less than five times while he and Shapiro conducted their rushed turnover last week—"but I hope to rectify that quickly. Admiral Rodriquez talked about my combat record, so I'll just talk about, well, me."

John swallowed. Why was his mouth suddenly dry? Oh, right. That was because he couldn't remember the smart words he'd written to come next.

Improvisation wasn't one of John's strengths. Even tactically, he liked to plan everything well ahead of time, or at least as much as he could. John was too realistic to think that was always possible, but damn it, he *had* planned this speech. He'd just swung and missed.

"I guess you could call me a navy brat, though I'm also an air force brat, courtesy of dual military parents who somehow made it work all the way to thirty years. Thankfully, they got out before I made lieutenant commander and it got really awkward. I chose submarines at first because neither of my parents did anything like them, and I already had an engineering degree, so I figured, how hard could nuke school be?"

That made all of his former officers from *Razorback* laugh; they knew him and knew how much he sucked at doing anything that remotely resembled homework. John grinned.

"I didn't tell my parents that I almost failed out of nuke school. I was one of those kids on remedial study who wasn't allowed to go on liberty for the last two months, and then the same thing happened to me at prototype. It turns out that nuclear engineering is pretty different from electrical engineering—not that I'd been an academic superstar at the Academy, either." John led the chuckles this time. "But I forged onward, got to my first boat, and realized that submarines were a lot more fun than school."

Should he say something about every boat he'd been on? John *had* spent the time to come up with a clever anecdote about each, but now he couldn't remember anything out than the *most disorganized navigator in the history of the navy* label his division officers on *John*

Warner smacked on him. Grimacing—and immediately hoping no one noticed it—John brushed that idea aside.

"A couple boats later, I found myself in command of *Cero*. I wasn't her first commanding officer, but I was lucky enough to get her after all the kinks were worn out. I thought I was done with command after her, and then I moved on to Admiral Jeff McNally's staff...and the First Battle of the SOM."

No one quite hissed, but there were whispers and ugly looks on dozens of faces in the crowd. None of the nastiness was pointed at John, but a lot of people in the navy lost friends that day...and since. History would forever record the First Battle of the Strait of Malacca as the opening act of World War III, and John had been right next to Jeff McNally as his admiral lost his cool and fired at a submarine before properly identifying it.

If a couple thousand Americans hadn't died that day, John would've said McNally got the spanking he deserved. Instead, McNally lived, three ships sank, and America marched into a war that was killing John's friends and colleagues left and right.

"That was a bad day," John said before he could stop himself. "Maybe the worst of my life. But some of the *Nereus* sailors in the audience will be relieved that I learned a couple of things about surface ships while I was embarked on *Enterprise*. First of all, I learned that you guys don't like to be called 'skimmers.'" A few chuckles broke through the grief and memories. "I also learned you *really* don't like subs calling you targets. Imagine that."

More laughter. "But the best lesson overall came on *Razorback*, the boat I didn't expect to command at all. See, I'd never really been on a tender before, except to visit one back in San Diego when I was a wee division officer. But on *Razorback*, we hooked up with a sub tender several times—including *Nereus*—and you guys kept us alive when it counted. I know being on a tender isn't a glamorous job. But sometimes, it's the people who quietly do what's got to be done that matter the most."

In that written speech, the one that John left back in the stinking hotel, there were some pretty words about service to country before self and all those things he learned at the Academy. But John's pounding head couldn't resurrect those sentences, so instead he forged forward more casually:

"Most of you are going to know your jobs better than I ever will. You're professionals, the best at what you do. I'm a pretty decent hand in an attack sub"—this time, the laughter was much louder—"but this tender thing will be new for me. I'll need you all to show me the way. In return, I'll do my best to keep this big lady both busy and floating. Doing our jobs might sometimes take us to ugly places, but from what Captain Shapiro here has told me, none of you are the type to skirt your duty."

Damn it, there was something else he wanted to say, but it felt just out of reach for his foggy brain. John was never going near adult beverages and Admiral Rodriquez at the same time again. "I am honored to come to *Nereus* and doubly so to replace so fine a captain."

Admiral Rodriquez stood up. "Thank you, Captain Dalton. Ladies and gentlemen, please rise for the reading of the orders.

"Attention to orders: To Captain John Dalton, from Commander Submarine Forces, Pacific Fleet. Assume duties as Commanding Officer, USS *Nereus*, AS Four-Three, on 11 October 2039."

He turned to Shapiro. "Captain Shapiro, are you ready to be relieved of command?"

She nodded once, sharply. "I am ready to be relieved, sir."

John turned and snapped off his sharpest salute. "I relieve you, ma'am."

"I stand relieved." Shapiro returned the salute.

Admiral Rodriquez smiled. "Ladies and gentlemen, I give you Captain John Dalton, Commanding Officer, USS *Nereus*."

John remembered preening as the official party departed when he took command of *Cero*. His change of command ceremony for *Razorback* had been much more rushed—and the man he was relieving much less dignified about it—but his hangover-addled brain seemed to think that it had done its one job and now it was done for the day. Thankfully, the ceremony for *Nereus* was an interesting mix of wartime streamlining and peacetime tradition, which made it hours shorter than it might have been.

Yet he was still expected to press flesh, shake hands, and make friends with all and sundry afterward. John was used to being good at that, but today he needed Janet running interference.

"You owe me, big boy," she muttered in his ear with a smile. "I've already talked three reporters into leaving you alone."

"I'll pay you back." He made a face. "Somehow."

"When do you get underway?"

"Tomorrow."

Janet sighed. "I suppose the eleven days we've gotten were the most we could expect at war." She shook herself. "I'm needed back in the plant, anyway. Those next-gen torpedoes won't design or test themselves."

"Something after the Mark 84?" John asked, fascination overriding the hangover.

"Not if they keep exploding in our tubes. We've got three different designs at Lazark, and I hear Pulsar's working on one or two also. But nothing yet."

"Pity."

"Less pity that you won't need them, at least from where I'm sitting," she replied.

"We do have over-the-side torpedo tubes, but I think I'll have to be pretty desperate to try them instead of depth charges." John chuckled. "I'd rather use neither, of course. *Nereus* is not made to dance in harm's way."

Janet eyed him. "You'd better keep that in mind, mister."

"Hey, I'm not some glory-hounding fool. I only ever take calculated risks, and I don't like taking on fights I don't think I can win."

"Thank God for small favors." She sighed. "At least we'll be able to talk more? Nancy says you should have good satellite connectivity on *Nereus.*"

"Andrea said the same, so looks like we'll have to work out a schedule for calls." John felt a smile tug at his tired face. "I'd like actually seeing your face and hearing your voice. Beats the hell out of emails."

"Beats the hell out of emails that get sent *weeks* after you write them, you mean." She punched him in the arm lightly.

"That's what I said, right?"

"Come on. That two-star admiral is gesturing us over, and you can't afford to ignore admirals."

Janet pulled John toward his next social engagement, and he grabbed a soda off a round serving table along the way. Sugary drinks were a quick way to make his midsection grow past the navy's antiquated height and weight standards...but John was pretty sure his Navy Cross would give him a pass on that. No one was going to kick the navy's best submariner out because of a bit of a belly, were they?

Nah. There was a war on, and he knew how to shoot. Even if he his new destiny was sitting in a lumbering tender, John still knew he was the best.

Chapter Seven

The Hunted

12 October 2039

I f there was one thing John could get used to quick on a surface
ship, it was seeing sunsets at sea. Sitting in a chair on the starboard
bridgewing, with his feet up and watching the sun set was a new
luxury...but one he was already in love with.

"Looks like our shakedown cruise just became something more,
Captain."

His new XO's voice made him jump. John turned to face Lieutenant Commander Arnie Quinn. Arnie was tall, and by which John
meant *really* tall. A former basketball player at the Naval Academy,
he was pushing six foot six, dark-skinned, narrow and well-muscled,
and he moved like a cat. He'd even gone pro for a year, before an ankle
injury took him out of the game for good, though from what John
heard, he still dominated pickup games on base. *Nereus'* sports teams
were some of the best in Perth, a fact that John found ridiculously
pleasing.

The fact that they wouldn't need John and his two left feet was even better. His sport at the Academy had been sailing, which didn't require running fast or kicking balls. John loved the sea and hated running, so sailing had been the best possible option.

"What happened?" John asked.

"*Sperry* went down this morning, sir." Arnie scowled. "Sounds like that French fucker got her."

A lead weight landed on John's chest. "Rochambeau?"

"That's the one." Arnie was a surface warfare officer; in the navy's infinite wisdom, the XO of a sub tender was always a surface guy to balance out the submariner in command. It was probably a good idea; John didn't find driving *Nereus* too different from a sub on the surface, but radars and fire control and close-in defense weapons were things he had limited experience with.

"So much for being free of him when I surfaced." John sighed. "Any survivors?"

"They got picked up by HMAS *Hobart* this morning. They never saw *Barracuda* coming." Arnie's eyes narrowed. "Asshole tweeted about it, though."

"I still can't understand the depth of ego required to do that." John shook his head. "And it's not that I lack ambition, but tweeting about sinking the enemy is a great way to send a posse of enemies on a hunt for you."

"Pity it hasn't worked on him."

"Got a copy of the tweet?" John gestured to the tablet in Arnie's hand.

"Yes, sir."

> **Captain Jules Rochambeau**
> **@JulesRochambeau**
> @USNavy should guard your submarine tenders better. Particularly when they have national assets alongside. Are you missing a ballistic missile submarine?
> **#barracuda #sperry #columbia #ssbn #war**

John noticed the hashtags and swore. "You didn't mention *Columbia*. Is there a SUBMISS/SUBSUNK buoy in message traffic?"

"No, sir." Arnie gulped. "I thought he was just trying to goad us."

"Maybe he is. But in my experience, that rat bastard usually doesn't have to lie."

Arnie blinked. "Is there anything we can do?"

"Not if he sank *Sperry* with *Columbia* alongside. Shit." John ran a hand through his thinning hair. "Catching a tender with a boomer alongside would be a hell of a prize. And if *Sperry* went down fast enough that *Columbia* couldn't get away..."

He swallowed, picturing what would happen if a massive sub tender like *Nereus* rolled over on a submarine. There'd be no hope for the boat, not if they had any open hatches—which they would if they were taking on weapons or stores. Was *Columbia* out here? John could shoot a message off to Admiral Rodriquez, who should know. But Uncle Marco would've seen the tweet, too. In fact, he probably got it faster than *Nereus,* since land internet was a lot faster than the slow satellites they shared out here.

John's chest was tight. The job of ballistic missile submarines was to remain in stealth until and unless their missiles were needed. Everyone hoped they would never be, which meant no one—even other American submarines—knew where they were hiding. *Columbia* was the lead ship of her class, only four years old and probably the quietest submarine ever made. Sailors joked that the best way to find a *Columbia*-class boat was to look for where the water was silent instead of trying to filter her ambient sounds out from the ocean life around her.

John had exercised against *Columbia* when in command of *Razorback*, and the jokes weren't wrong. The only way he'd ever caught the missile boat was when she was on her way to the surface or submerging. Otherwise, that boat was as quiet as a grave.

Ouch. That was a bad analogy.

"What would you like to do, Captain?" Arnie asked. His face was tight. Did he expect John—the best living Alliance submariner—to want to run toward a fight?

The thought almost made John laugh. How ridiculous would he look, trying to run to the rescue in his gargantuan tender with her max speed of twenty-five knots? He was lucky she could go that fast. Past sub tenders made do with speeds of five knots less in a following current.

"Keep our eyes peeled and sonar manned. If we find survivors, we pick them up. Not much else we can do from here, is there?" John replied.

"No, sir, not really." Arnie had the grace to look ashamed.

"You said our shakedown cruise got cut short. What's the mission now?"

"Christmas Island. We're scheduled to rendezvous with HMS *Ajax* along the way and give her a torpedo reload at sea. That will be complex."

"It was hairy when I got one from you folks on *Razorback*." John grimaced. "Made me swear never to do it again. Can we at least find the lee of some island or another?"

"Not much between here and Christmas Island, sir."

"Of course there isn't." John sat back in his chair. "Well, then in that case—and since the Brits like formality—send the captain of *Ajax* my regards and—"

"Captain, Sonar is reporting a submerged contact at medium range," the officer of the deck leaned into the bridgewing to report. Lieutenant (junior grade) Lisa Cunningham was young, freckled, and had hair shorter than John's, but she seemed pretty sharp. "No classification yet. CIC recommends streaming the tail."

"Stream the tail," John ordered and then thought about it for a moment. "But keep it at a short stay. I don't want to go flinging depth charges around if it's out a mile behind us."

"Stream the tail to a short stay, aye!" Cunningham disappeared back into the bridge.

Nereus' "tail," or Tactical Towed Sonar Array, was similar to the one he'd had on *Razorback,* albeit longer. The TACTAS, informally called the "tail," was a mile of hydrophones that a ship or submarine could trail behind it to extend their passive sonar listening envelope. In a ship's case, it also dipped those hydrophones deeper into a submarine's operating environment, getting them clear of the ship's own noises—such as engine sounds, propellers turning, and miscellaneous equipment noises—so the sonar team could create a better contact picture.

By their very nature, submarines could "see" the underwater sonar landscape better than a surface ship; while a ship sailed *on* the sea, a submarine was *in* it. John had taken ruthless advantage of that fact dozens of times while an attack submarine commander, but now he found himself on the other foot.

He was not enjoying the experience.

"What are you thinking, Captain?" Arnie's eyes were a little wide, and John remembered that *Nereus* hadn't seen much combat under Shapiro. Their first defense had always been to run away.

"I'm thinking that the best defense is sometimes a good offense." John shrugged. "Unless that's a diesel boat out there, or unless it's a friendly, we don't have much chance in a race. Every enemy SSN is faster than we are, and so are their torpedoes. I know. I was chasing *them* two weeks ago." He made himself sit back in his chair and think. "So we have to play it smart. Find them first and then fling depth charges at them to make them think about staying alive instead of killing us."

Arnie gulped. "Does that work, sir?"

"It worked on me."

Hopping out of his chair, John strode into the bridge, expecting the buzz of activity that he would've encountered on *Razorback*. But *Nereus's* bridge was still quiet, with only the officer of the deck talking to the combat information center over the centerline intercom.

Right. CIC was in a compartment aft of the bridge. Surface ships split up navigation and tactical operations, though John didn't quite understand why. Maybe it was because it got so damned dark out at night?

Submarines tried to avoid running on the surface in the dark. For one, it was an easy way to get run over by a ship that didn't see you, and two, subs were more efficient in every way when submerged. Surface ships, on the other hand, didn't exactly get to pick. John made a face.

"XO, let's set battle—crap, what do you guys call it?"

"General Quarters, Captain."

Yet another thing that was different for no reason. John sucked in a deep breath. "Set general quarters."

"Set general quarters, aye! Boats!" Arnie turned to the boatswain's mate of the watch, who immediately grabbed the handset for the 1MC, or general announcing system, as the donging of the general alarm filled the air.

"General Quarters, General Quarters. All hands, man your battle stations. The route of travel is forward and up to starboard, down and aft to port. Set material condition Zebra throughout the ship. Reason for General Quarters: potential enemy submarine contact."

John ignored the repetition of the words and avoided a rushing sailor to slip over to Arnie's side. "How do you usually swing this?" he asked. "You stay on the bridge and I cover CIC?"

The whites in Arnie's eyes seemed to glow in the darkening bridge. "Yes, sir."

"Then you've got the bridge. I'll be back aft." John matched actions to words and headed to CIC, glad that it was only two compartments aft of the bridge. When he entered the space, an immediate feeling of familiarity swept through him.

The ship's bridge was almost an alien environment. It was nothing like the narrow confines of a submarine's sail—which they called the bridge—or the control room on *Razorback*. But CIC, the Combat Information Center, felt almost like control. Consoles framed the room, full of radar, electronic warfare, weapons control, and sonar displays. Seated sailors wore headsets while they focused on their screens, watching for the enemy. The only difference was the lights, which were blue on *Nereus*. Submarines kept their lights white or red. What was with the blue?

John decided that now was not the time to ask. At least he had fought in a CIC environment before; the flag bridge on *Enterprise* had looked much like this. Squaring his shoulders, he slipped between two sailors and the chart table to reach the captain's chair at the front of the space.

Nereus' CIC watch officer, or CICWO, looked up at him. "Good evening, sir. Still prosecuting the potential submerged contact. Likely bearing zero-niner-one at fifteen nautical miles."

"Thank you." John slipped into the chair, eyeing the officer to his right.

That seat *should* belong to his operations officer, but Lieutenant Castro was on medical leave. Instead, his young weapons officer, Lieutenant (junior grade) Kyou Maeda, sat in the chair. Maeda was only on his second division officer tour, and John knew nothing aside from his name and that he was a graduate of the Virginia Military Institute. He looked impossibly young in the watch officer's chair, and John hoped to hell Maeda knew what he was doing.

"The tail should settle out in fifteen minutes, sir," Maeda said.

"Very well."

The wait was interminable. John pulled up information on *Nereus'* weapons capabilities while he waited, but there was nothing in the computer that he hadn't learned in his turnover from Captain Shapiro.

Nereus, like all of her sisters, wasn't a warship designed for a standup fight. She had self-defense weapons, but not much else. She had two eight-pack launchers for RIM-162 Evolved Sea Sparrow Missiles (ESSM), which could be used against either surface or air targets. She also had two Block 2B CIWS gun mounts for close-in air defense. John hoped he'd never need those; *Nereus* had no business in an air battle or getting missiles shot at her.

She was far more likely to need her two over-the-side torpedo launchers, each of which carried four torpedoes and could be reloaded by the ever-reliable Mark 84 ASV. Those damn things had a near twenty percent failure rate in John's last battle on *Razorback*, but they were the best anti-submarine weapon in his navy's arsenal...maybe.

Nereus also belonged to one of the few classes of ships who carried *four* Mark 20 Hedgehog launchers. For almost a century, the U.S. Navy had believed depth charges—rocket propelled or otherwise—were a thing of the past, but this war proved otherwise. Surface ships could sink subs, or at least scare them off, with depth charges, which was why *Nereus* carried four launchers, each of which bristled with thirty mini-missiles, each of which had a range of seven-point-five nautical miles and could be set to explode at any depth up to a mile deep.

Surface ship drivers tended to shoot torpedoes first. They were smart and quick, and they'd been America's weapon of choice for ninety years. Having been on the receiving end of more than one depth charging, John felt he had a greater appreciation for depth charges than any bean counter back in Washington. Those Hedgehogs might be a redesign of a *really* old weapon, but they were reliable, and they were damned useful.

"CICWO, Sonar Sup, preliminary identification track six-zero-five-five. Tonals correspond to *Akula* II or III class submarine. Unsure if Russian or Indian. Recommend redesignating as track seven-zero-five-five and declaring hostile."

"CICWO, aye and concur, break, Captain."

"Captain, aye. Redesignate as hostile. Range?" A rush of adrenaline swept down John's spine, and he felt himself sit up straighter.

"Captain, Sonar, approximately twenty-five thousand yards."

John cocked his head, thinking. Twenty-five thousand yards was twelve-point-five nautical miles. That was well within the range for a Mark 84 ASV torpedo. Maybe his initial thoughts had been wrong.

"Do you have a strong enough sonar contact for a firing solution?" John asked.

"Negative, sir. Holding this guy on passive is hard."

John gritted his teeth, glancing at Maeda. "And the moment we go active, he knows everything about us, right down to our underwear size."

Maeda blinked. "I know active sonar works both ways, sir, but it isn't that bad, is it?"

"Weps, if I was that *Akula*, I'd be *praying* we'd go active." John scowled at his own display for a moment. "Come on. Take a walk with me."

Maeda looked at him like he'd grown a second head right out of his ass, but John was the captain, so he followed when John took him over to the sonar corner. Fortunately, Chief Asher, the sonar supervisor, seemed much less surprised to see them.

"Crappy sonar conditions, Chief?" John asked.

"How'd you guess, Captain?" Chief Asher was a sonar technician (surface), but he looked a lot like every sonar tech John ever worked with. He had a Twizzler in one hand and a grease pencil in the other, and his glasses were thick due to too much time staring at the screen.

John shrugged. "If they were better, that *Akula* would've shot us already. Instead, he's creeping up close to make sure we're worth the effort."

"Worth the effort?" Maeda's frown made him look like a high school student.

"Everyone's in a pinch over torpedoes. No one's got enough, even the enemy. The Indians are less put out than the Russians, but this *Akula* could be either one. The Russians build them and sell them to India, and now they've sent India the plans and tech reps to build them, too," John replied. "No submariner wants to pop a torpedo into a civilian ship when they might find a warship right over the horizon and then be out of torps."

"Don't they just want to sink ships?"

"We generally want to sink the *right* ships," John said. "But sonar's the only eyes we have. Unless this guy gets dumb enough to pop his scope up and take a look around. Then we'll get him on radar, and he's toast."

Chief Asher grinned. "How do you want to bag him, sir?"

"Only way we can. We play fat, dumb, and happy until he gets close enough to kill." John grimaced. "Hopefully, you get a good enough track on him that we can shoot a couple of torpedoes his way. If we don't, we creep along and drop depth charges on his head when he gets too close."

"The Hedgehog has a *third* of our torpedo's range, Captain," Maeda whispered, pasty-faced.

"Welcome to the big leagues, Weps." John made himself smile.

Surface ships weren't his game, but he knew what to do with combat. And John had a pretty good idea what the enemy submarine captain was thinking, because that had been him less than two weeks earlier. Would his guesses be right? There was only one way to find out.

Chapter Eight

Turning the Tables

L etting an enemy get close had never been John's favorite tactic, mostly because it took the initiative out of his hands and put it right where he didn't want it: the enemy's. However, today, his choices were limited, so he would take the best option out of a load of bad ones.

Back on *Razorback,* John had always been the hunter. Not once had he let an enemy creep up on him. But on *Nereus*...it seemed he had to play a different game.

Scowling, he slumped in his captain's chair and watched time tick by and the *Akula* creep closer. Even with the tail out, *Nereus's* track on the *Akula* was not very strong. They could see the enemy, but shooting a torpedo that way could be wasteful. Particularly if John pickled off two like he wanted to.

"How many Mark 84s do we have on board, Weps?" he asked Maeda, mostly to keep the kid thinking.

His weapons officer wasn't a bad officer, but this was his first wartime deployment as a junior department head, and it showed. On a warship like *Razorback*, the weapons officer was a full lieutenant—sometimes a lieutenant commander—but here on *Nereus*, where Weps's main job was to arm up visiting submarines, the billet belonged to a lieutenant junior grade on his second sea tour. Maeda served as an engineer on an amphibious warship during his first tour, and while he had a few exciting stories about dropping marines off to fight over underwater stations...it wasn't exactly the same.

Particularly not when Maeda experienced that excitement while staring at a screen in the engineering plant.

John managed not to sigh as Maeda pulled up numbers on his computer. That was the kind of metric any good weapons officer had memorized, but he had to give the kid a chance. Maeda had reported on board just two weeks before John, and the officer he replaced left just three days earlier. Maeda was so new that John was surprised he knew which ammunitions locker stored which weapons.

Maybe he didn't know. John didn't intend to ask.

"Eighty-seven, sir.

John frowned. "Including those in the launchers?"

"Oh. No, sir. Those are the ones we have in stock for replenishments." Maeda chewed his lip. "We could use them in our own over-the-side launchers, I suppose. I'm not sure we have an underway reloading procedure, but..."

He trailed off when John held up a hand. "No need. That answers my question."

Scratching an ear, John stared at the big screen plot and weighed his options. The only good news was how the *Akula* continued to close the range. The enemy sub was now eight nautical miles away and still gaining on *Nereus*, helped by the sub tender's slight decrease in speed.

John hadn't wanted to make it obvious that he wanted to be caught, but continuing on at eighteen knots would've made the chase take all night, and he really wanted to get some sleep.

He glanced at the clock. It was almost twenty-two hundred, or ten at night to a civilian, in their time zone. John was dead tired, and that damned *Akula* still wasn't in range. John wasn't a numbers wizard, but nine knots of overtake made for pretty simple math. The *Akula* maintained a hair above her best silent speed of twenty-three knots, probably assuming a sub tender wasn't listening too closely. *Nereus* had slowed to fifteen knots—as slow as John dared, to better make himself look like a bumbling idiot—thus giving the enemy that precious nine knots of speed to catch up to him.

The range crept down with all the grace of a slow faucet leak. Four hours after detecting the enemy submarine, they were still eight miles apart.

"Captain, Sonar, positive I.D. on track seven-zero-five-five. Tonals match an *Akula III* across the board. Contact is Indian, sir."

John smashed the foot pedal to activate his headset microphone a little too hard in excitement; it was nice to finally get some news! "Captain, aye."

Now if only they'd stumble into depth charge range...

"Sir, we're inside their torpedo range." Maeda gripped a rag in his hands, twisting it back and forth. "Doesn't matter if they carry TEST 83s or Black Sharks. Either way, they can shoot us from here."

"Kyou, they could've shot us five miles ago." John felt more relaxed now that action was imminent. "Much like us, the Indians don't like shooting from outside ten thousand yards. Too much inaccuracy in modern torpedoes."

Maeda frowned. "I thought modern torpedoes were smart."

"They're smarter than the ones used in World War II, sure, but they're still pretty dumb if you can't guide them in. And the TEST 83 has proven less dependable than most. There's a reason why we fear Jules Rochambeau more than Avani Patel."

"Surface ship drivers have to fear all of them, sir."

John chuckled. "Noted. But this guy is cautious. He wants his kill. Maybe we're his first, or maybe he just doesn't want to waste torpedoes. Either way, it's going to doom him."

"What if he gets a shot off?"

"Then the XO drives *Nereus* until the screws fall off or the torpedo hits." John knew that the first time getting shot at was the worst...and at least this wasn't an air battle. Those terrified him more than any number of torpedoes. "Start warming up your Hedgehogs, please."

"Warm up the Hedgehogs, aye. How big of a salvo size do you want, Captain?"

"Full spread along his bearing, and then two more, each offset fifteen degrees to port and starboard, thirty seconds later."

"Weps, aye." Maeda sounded more confident now that he had work to do. Maybe John had misjudged him.

Or he'd have to hold his hand through the entire engagement. Ah, well. Not the first time. Speaking of people who had done less than overwhelm him with their competence, John grabbed a phone and called the bridge.

Lieutenant Commander Arnie Quinn picked up on the first ring. "XO."

"Arnie, it's the captain. Our customer's almost in range, so it's about time to drop some depth charges on his head. Prep the bridge watch team to run like mad if he throws a torpedo at us, and make sure you have the noisemakers ready. I can say from experience that noisemakers work as well as, if not better than, maneuvering against the TEST 83 torpedo."

"Sir, are you sure that suckering this *Akula* in is the right thing to do? We sub tenders...well, we don't *do* that," Arnie replied.

"Is that why everyone's looking at me so strangely?" John asked.

"Probably."

"Well, it's too late now. He's eight miles away and sonar conditions are crummy, but not bad enough for him to lose us if we speed up, so we're stuck with trying to sink him."

"If you say so, sir." Arnie's voice shook like a sheep on the way to slaughter.

"Remember your training, follow your checklists, and you'll do fine." John wished he'd had more time to drill *Nereus'* crew, but Andrea Shapiro said they aced every drill she threw at them.

Had she done nothing other than fire drills and abandon ship drills? John swallowed the urge to ask. He didn't want to know.

"I'll let the bridge team know, Captain." Arnie sounded a touch more confident, but John wasn't about to write home in joy. Not yet.

"Thank you," he said, and hung up. Then he grabbed the microphone for the general announcing system from its cradle on his right. He had to give it to surface ships; they made good use of all their extra *space* by having well-laid-out consoles with everything useful in easy reach. John cleared his throat.

"Evening, *Nereus*, this is the captain. As you know, we've been playing possum and waiting for an enemy submarine to get close enough for us to kill it. Well, our patience has paid off. This Indian *Akula* is almost close enough for us to depth charge into oblivion. Now, I know some of you—like me—are submariners. You might've experienced depth charging before and wanted to wish it on your worst enemy.

Today's the day. Once this guy gets close enough, our Hedgehogs are going to rain explosions down on their heads.

"I know this is new for some of you, but we've all trained for this. Keep your heads about you. Trust each other. You're in the best navy in the world and on the best damned ship you could hope for. We'll get through it together. Dalton, out."

John snuck a glance at Maeda, who wore a slight smile after that speech, and resisted the urge to preen. He was decent at pre-battle speeches, as he should be. John had a lot of practice.

"CICWO, Sonar Sup, the *Akula* has dipped below the layer, but I still have a slight track on him. Range now seven-point-five nautical miles."

"Watch Officer, aye," Maeda replied and then twisted to look at John. "Ready, sir?"

John contemplated letting the *Akula* get a little closer, to shorten the range between the enemy boat and his ship so that he could send *more* salvos of depth charges at him in case the first ones missed. Yet *Nereus* was an untried ship with a nervous crew...best he play it smart.

"FIS is green," John announced, turning the firing key to his right from *red* to *green*, which released control of *Nereus'* weapons. "Weapons Officer, you have batteries release on the pre-briefed firing plan."

"Weps, aye!" Maeda's voice went high, but his hands were steady as he hit the buttons. "Full spread of hedgehogs launching in three—two—one—*launch!*"

On *Nereus'* stern, the port Hedgehog launcher twisted to the *Akula's* bearing and shot off eight mini-missiles in quick succession. Eight rocket-propelled depth charges made for a full spread; while each Hedgehog could be loaded with up to forty-eight depth charges at one time, that meant they didn't need to be reloaded until after six spreads were launched.

Nereus had four Hedgehog launchers. She hadn't been designed with any, but war had a tendency to change technology quickly. Detractors claimed that reverting to depth charges was like rewriting ancient history, but as a submariner, John could testify to their deadliness. He didn't care that the United States stopped building depth charges early in the Cold War. Their *enemies* hadn't, and the Indians and Russians both used them with devastating effectiveness in the early days of the war. He might never know how many friends he lost to depth charges, only that dozens of American submarines had been felled by them.

Now it was his turn.

The eight miniature missiles arched into the sky, sailing through the air at nearly Mach 1. They entered the water a little more than seven miles astern of the submarine tender, sank to their preprogrammed depth, and exploded in a circular-shaped pattern.

John could imagine the jarring concussions on the *Akula*, could almost feel the way the Indian submarine rocked and shook with the impacts. How far away were they? He had no way to know. Then, thirty seconds after the first explosives entered the water, the second and third salvos—this time from both Hedgehog launchers—followed, offset to each side in case the *Akula* dodged left or right.

"Launch transients!" Chief Asher's voice boomed out over the internal network. "Launch transients bearing zero-niner-niner!"

John stomped the foot pedal so hard his foot cracked. "Conn—shit, *Bridge*, Captain, torpedo in the water. Commence evasive maneuvering."

The palms of his hands were sweaty. This surface stuff was for the birds; John couldn't drive the ship away from the threat here in CIC, not like he could on a submarine. He had to trust his bridge crew and his XO to do the job...but were they up to it?

God, he hoped Andrea Shapiro had been telling the truth about how hard she drilled them.

"Bridge, aye, break Central, coming to flank," Arnie replied immediately.

"Central, aye," *Nereus's* chief engineer replied on the same net.

Holding his breath, John watched the red upside-down icon representing an enemy torpedo blink to life on the plot. *Please be a TEST 83,* he didn't dare whisper out loud. Sailors didn't like to hear their CO whispering prayers, but if this was a newer and faster torpedo...*Nereus* was screwed.

A TEST 83 could still kill them, of course. It was a fast torpedo at fifty-five knots, and *Nereus* wasn't far enough away to run it out of gas. But if they could drop noisemakers at the right time and confuse it, even India's best torpedo might do donuts *looking* for them until it exhausted its fuel and dropped to the ocean floor.

Nereus trembled, her twin screws cutting into the water and her diesel engines straining as she sprinted to her top speed of twenty-five knots. John felt her leaning out of her port turn as she turned away from the torpedo, and he hoped to hell that Arnie and the bridge team dropped the first noisemaker at the right point on the turn. He could ask, but he knew he shouldn't. Arnie was a surface warfare officer and knew how to drive *Nereus* better than John did.

No, John should concentrate on sinking the damned *Akula* before it got another shot off.

One torpedo was a snapshot. That was the fish any sane sub CO kept ready in a tube, the one set to fire at any enemy who attacked unexpectedly. The fact that more torpedoes weren't incoming meant the *Akula* hadn't been ready to kill *Nereus,* at least not yet.

But that Indian CO had just gotten a *lot* more motivated, so it was time for John to do him or her in first.

"Sonar, Captain, any further launches?"

"Negative. Torpedo bears zero-one-zero, range fourteen thousand yards and closing at five-five knots."

"Captain, aye. Any breakup noises on the *Akula*?"

The silence was too long; John twisted in his seat to look back toward the trio of sonar stations, where Chief Archer was now hunched over one of his operators, whispering furiously. Immediately, his heart sank.

He knew what had happened. He'd seen it from rookie sonar operators on *Razorback* at the war's start, too—once a torpedo entered the water, every available sonar tech put their ears on that contact and forgot the true danger: the sub that shot at them. After all, a single torpedo could only kill them once. That *Akula* carried forty such opportunities to sink *Nereus*.

"Captain, Sonar, negative breakup noises. Track seven-zero-five-five moving from right to left, new bearing one-one-four."

"Estimated depth?" John asked.

"Uncertain, likely deeper than our depth charges."

"Punch it in, Weps. One pattern on the bearing at five hundred feet, then two more with a fifteen-degree offset to either side set for two thousand feet," John ordered.

"Two thousand, sir?" Maeda's eyes went wide. "Isn't that the test depth for an *Akula* III?"

"It's where I'd go if I was him."

Something in John's voice made Maeda's nod grow firm. "Hedgehog patterns programmed, Captain."

"Hit it."

Maeda's finger stabbed down on the touchscreen. "Fourth salvo away!" Then, thirty seconds later, just as *Nereus* leaned out of her next turn, he added: "Salvos five and six launched!"

"Very well." John took a deep breath and returned his attention to the torpedo icon on the screen. With its thirty knots of overtake, that torpedo would hit them in less than thirteen minutes if they couldn't outfox it.

Damn. Quick math told John that plus the time the torpedo had already been in the water was *just* less than the TEST 83's runtime of fourteen minutes, ten seconds at its max speed. He'd have to do this the hard way and evade. Granted, if the Indian CO was clever and had kept the torpedo on the wire, he or she could slow it down to get more time in the water...but that was unlikely. Snapshots were generally fire-and-forget weapons, and the explosions near the *Akula* probably would've snapped any control wire, anyway.

So far, that was the one factor in John's favor. Could he figure out how to maximize that?

"All stations, Sonar, explosions bearing zero-one-four, *big* explosions. I think we got him!" Chief Archer's voice was jubilant, and a couple people cheered.

"Settle down, people!" John cut in. "We still have a torpedo in the water, and a dead sub can kill us if we're careless. Keep your heads about you, and we can celebrate later."

"Sonar, aye." Chief Asher sounded abashed, but John didn't have time to reassure him.

"Good job, Weps," he said to Maeda. "Tell your people that, too. I'm heading to the bridge."

"Thank you, sir." Maeda's previously nervous expression was gone; the praise made him glow as John clapped him on the shoulder.

John stumbled getting out of his chair, swore, and sprinted for the bridge. He had to fight to get CIC's watertight hatch open as *Nereus* rolled into another turn, and then he bounced off a bulkhead on his way forward to the bridge. Damn, surface ships swayed more than submarines.

Ignoring the first flush of seasickness bubbling in his gut, John made it through the aft doors to the bridge just as Arnie announced, "Fourth noisemaker deployed!"

"Hard left rudder!" Lieutenant (junior grade) Lisa Cunningham ordered.

"Hard left rudder, aye! My rudder is left thirty-five degrees, no new course given," the sailor at the helm replied.

John needed a moment to orient himself; a surface ship's bridge at battle stations—no, *general quarters*, he corrected himself—was busy. The XO was out on the bridge wing while the officer of the deck stood centerline, and another officer stood behind the sailors at the helm and lee helm to ensure they didn't miss any orders. There were phone talkers in both corners, extra quartermasters, the navigator, and gunners on the fifty-caliber machine guns on both bridge wings.

Holy cow, what a way to run a railroad. Shaking himself, John slammed the watertight door shut and dogged it down.

"Captain on the bridge!" The officer behind the helm noticed him first.

"Carry on," John said, making his way forward against the sloping deck as *Nereus* turned.

"Rudder amidships!" Cunningham said, her eyes on the course indicator.

"Rudder amidships, aye."

"How are we looking, XO?" John asked as Arnie Quinn pulled another countermeasure free of its canister on the starboard bridgewing.

"Running like a rabid dog's on our heels, Captain." Arnie smiled, much to John's surprise. Maybe he had more of a spine than John thought. "Glad to hear we sank the *Akula.*"

"Me, too."

"All stations, Sonar, torpedo is turning!" Chief Archer's voice rang out of the speaker on the bridgewing bulkhead. "I say again, torpedo is turning with the noisemaker!"

"Make another turn now. Reciprocal from the last one and drop another noisemaker," John said, speaking to Arnie because he still wasn't qualified to drive his new ship...and Arnie clearly knew what to do with his big lady.

"OOD, come hard left!" Arnie snapped, hustling to the opposite bridge wing with the noisemaker in his hands.

It was amazing how much good a foot-long canister could do, but John knew those noisemakers well. Submarines used similar ones, only theirs were launched pneumatically. All the canisters did was dance and drop masses of continuous bubbles, making noise to confuse acoustic and wake-homing torpedoes.

Distracting a torpedo was both the simplest tactic and one of the hardest to pull off. Technology to "shoot down" an enemy torpedo the way the navy did missiles didn't exist yet, so submarines and surface ships alike had to provide a different target to divert the torpedo long enough that its original target got out of range. Once the torpedo finished circling the countermeasure and looked for a new target, all John could do was hope *Nereus* would be out of its detection range.

Or, in the situation where a torpedo like the TEST 83 had little enough gas at its top speed, he could hope it would run out of gas before it could get to him, even if it tried chasing his ship again. Still, that meant getting the hell away from the torpedo as fast as they could.

"Countermeasure away!" Arnie chucked the last noisemaker over the side as *Nereus* turned again.

"Is there any reason those things are still launched manually?" John asked.

Arnie frowned. "Is there another way?"

"Yeah, on subs we hit a button."

"Huh." Arnie blinked. "I guess you can't take a quick walk outside, can you?"

"No, not really." John chuckled. "Good job up here. Looks like all I could do was provide moral support."

"Torpedo evasion is something we drilled until our eyes bled, Captain," Arnie replied. Then his eyes drifted back aft. "I think we should probably come up with some Hedgehog tactics, though. I was listening on net fifteen, and I don't think we have any procedure to cover the tactics you used."

John leaned against the railing as *Nereus* steadied out, still running at full speed to put as much distance between herself and the torpedo as possible. Arnie wasn't wrong; Cunningham knew her stuff. "You mean *Nereus* doesn't have procedures, or the surface navy doesn't?"

"Probably both. Depth charges aren't really our thing." Arnie grimaced. "My last ship was a destroyer, and we never touched the things."

"Sounds like we need to call the Aussies up and take notes. They're good at it." John rubbed his neck. "So're the Indians, but obviously, I'm not asking them."

Arnie barked out a laugh. "No, sir. Let's not."

"Speaking of the Indians, we should loop around and see if there are any survivors off that *Akula* once the torpedo dies," John said.

"Come again?"

"If you hit the roof right before the water comes in, your people have a chance." John grimaced. "We watched a lot of video recordings from sunken subs before we started realizing that was the only way to get anyone off. If you know it's going to hit, do an emergency blow. You'll still lose your boat, but some of your crew might still get off."

"You...you want to pick them up after they almost killed us?" Arnie stared at John like he was speaking another language.

Maybe he was. John shrugged.

"Someone should, and we're the only ones nearby. Besides, making them POWs means the Indians don't pop them in another boat so they can take *another* shot at us."

"Huh. I suppose I can get behind that, sir."

Chapter Nine

Unexpected Guests

R unning the Indian torpedo out of gas took another ten minutes; John waited five after that *just* to make sure he wasn't sailing his shiny new ship into a death trap. Then he looped *Nereus* around, posting extra lookouts and approaching the *Akula's* last known position at fifteen knots.

John had never enjoyed watching the VDR, or Video Data Recorder, footage uploaded to the SUBMISS/SUBSUNK buoy by a sinking submarine. But there were lessons learned to be found there, so he always steeled himself and did it, anyway, encouraging his senior officers on *Razorback* to do it, too. He knew some captains thought it was bad luck, but watching the mistakes others made taught John how to stay alive.

It had also showed him the one way to survive if his boat got hit, which was the method he'd described to Arnie earlier. By luck, skill, or the grace of God, he'd never needed to use that knowledge, but it still rattled around his skull now that he was on a surface ship. So did the fact that many subs "automatically" launching life rafts got hung up—or straight-up destroyed—in the explosions that sank the boats. Today, that meant he knew to look for people bobbing in the water instead of bright orange life rafts.

"You sure anyone could get off, sir?" Lieutenant (junior grade) Maeda asked, standing to John's right with a pair of binoculars.

They leaned over the starboard bridgewing together, searching the horizon now that Maeda had been relieved in CIC. The weapons officer had volunteered to help, his confidence clearly buoyed by their success sinking the *Akula*. His newfound self-assurance made John smile, even if the question didn't.

"I'm not prepared to discount the possibility until we check," he replied. "Every mariner knows our worst enemy is the sea itself, and now that we've dumped them into the water, we have a moral obligation to pick them up if we can."

"I just mean that we launched the last spreads at the *Akula's* test depth, sir. There was no way they could get to the surface fast enough from there."

"Yeah, but we don't know *which* spread got them, Weps. If it was the five hundred footer, they could've lived." John grimaced. "Worst case, all we waste is some time."

"And gas, sir."

"Right." John chuckled. "I'm not used to tracking that."

One of the advantages to being a nuclear submariner was never having to refuel the reactor, at least not in a conventional way. During his turnover, John had been horrified upon learning *Nereus* measured fuel consumption in *gallons per mile* instead of the other way around, and reassurances from Andrea Shapiro that it was normal for surface ships did nothing to make him feel better. However, *Nereus* carried what John felt was an ungodly amount of fuel in her tanks, over four hundred thousand gallons of diesel fuel, maritime, so John figured if he burned a few hundred gallons looking for stranded sailors, he would be fine.

Besides, without life rafts or other flotation devices, John knew sailors wouldn't last long in the water. Maybe not even long enough for *Nereus* to reach them. But John had to try.

The minutes marched by with aching slowness. John and his team continued scanning the horizon, with every spare set of eyes looking for the *Akula's* survivors. Then, just as John started to lose hope, a sailor on the port bridgewing shouted:

"There! I see a life raft!"

John rushed to the opposite bridgewing with Maeda and the officer of the deck on his heels, training his binoculars on the bearing the young sailor indicated. It took him seconds to pick up the orange life raft bobbing in the sea.

Orange was a common color for life rafts; the Indian Navy used rafts with a dark orange bottom and a lighter orange top while the U.S. Navy used ones with a black bottom and orange top, but they were both visible against the vast blueness of the ocean. What John didn't expect was how *small* the life raft was; it looked about a third of the size of the ones he was used to. Squinting, he looked at the water around the raft.

"Are those people in the water?" he asked.

Maeda chewed his lip. "I think so, sir."

John grabbed his radio. "XO, Captain, stand by for recovery operations, port side!"

"XO copies." Arnie was already down on the boat deck, ready to supervise launching the boat and rigging ladders over the side. He'd organized that operation efficiently, which left John feeling guilty for thinking Arnie might not be up to his job earlier.

"OOD, kick up the speed and get us to those survivors pronto," John ordered.

"OOD, aye," Cunningham replied, passing orders to the helm to speed up to twenty-five knots.

Then all John could do was wait.

Ten minutes later, *Nereus* coasted down in speed a mere hundred feet from the clump of survivors, launching her port side small boat as she did. John didn't think of putting the starboard side boat in the water until it was too late; by then, all of his boatswain's mates were focused on lowering the ladders and preparing to receive survivors.

Meanwhile, John tried not to pace on the bridge. He was new at this; rescuing survivors wasn't really a submarine thing, though for all that he knew his friend Alex Coleman had pulled it off a few times. No one in their right mind would pull *enemy* sailors onto a submarine, however, which meant this experience would be a little...different.

That was why he ended up pulling out the satellite phone and calling up his new boss, Commodore Amanda Madison. He'd worked with her a few times when in command of *Razorback* and found "Grandma" Madison the logical and level-headed sort. She didn't deserve the nickname the late Kurt Kins had pegged on her, but it stuck, anyway. Things like that happened in the sub force.

Fortunately, her yeoman answered on the second ring and put John through right away.

"John?" Madison's voice was scratchy but audible, probably the best connection John could expect from a thousand miles away and a satellite connection. Luckily, the Indians hadn't started shooting down satellites in this part of the world; really, no one had tried that tactic yet.

John wondered which side would start first. Or was this war too civilized?

"Afternoon, Commodore. Sorry for the unexpected call, but *Nereus* just had a little mix up with an Indian *Akula*."

"Holy Jesus." Her voice cracked. "How many did you get off?"

"Say again?"

"Obviously, you survived. How many crew did you lose?" Madison asked. "Bad luck that one came after you on your first underway."

John laughed. "I'm sorry. I wasn't clear. We sank the *Akula*. I'm calling you because I'm about to pick up their survivors, and although my XO pulled up the SOP for this, I'd like to know where you want me to take them."

Silence came from the other end.

"Commodore? Did I lose you?"

"Damn it, John, don't scare me like that. Next time lead with you *sinking* the *Akula*."

"My apologies." John felt himself flush. "I'm used to the inference being me talking means that we survived the encounter."

Madison laughed. "Yes, you're still an attack boat jockey at heart. Neat trick, sinking an *Akula* with a tender. I'm sure Admiral Rodriquez will crow about you, and we'll throw another medal at you for it, too."

"Ma'am, it's the living part I like." John had never been accused of an excess of modesty, and he didn't *mind* getting medals—every one of them helped on his route to earning his own stars, and his own squadron like Commodore Madison commanded—but he wasn't egotistical enough to ignore the fact that sinking the enemy in wartime was his job.

"Then be careful with those survivors. You never know when one of them might get frisky and decide they don't want to be a POW."

"I've got a brig and intend to use it if any get rowdy. My weapons officer is working on the security watchbill now, too."

"Excellent." Madison took a deep breath. "As for where to take them...Christmas Island is a good bet. You're headed that direction, anyway, and we can fly them anywhere from there."

"Where do we keep prisoners of war these days?"

"Need to know, Captain," she replied.

"Christmas Island, aye, ma'am." John wasn't bothered by the rebuff; sometimes, the navy decided he didn't need to know things, and that was okay with him.

Peering over the side, he watched as *Nereus'* small boat—a fourteen-passenger RHIB, or rigid-hulled inflatable boat—collected survivors out of the water. Those who could swim well enough were climbing the ladders hanging down *Nereus'* side while the boat aimed for those further out. The life raft would be left for last, John imagined; the sailors in there were safest.

"Good job on the *Akula*, John. I look forward to reading about it in your report."

He chuckled. "And here I thought I was free of patrol reports when I turned over *Razorback*."

"Good try, but no."

"I'll get right on it, Commodore." John managed to keep his grimace out of his tone. Without Pat to help, he knew his patrol reports would be messy, late, and shorter than his boss wanted.

Organization remained his one great weakness, the thing he couldn't conquer without help. Was Arnie up to the task? John wasn't sure. He'd have to ask.

"I'm late to a meeting. Take care, John."

"You too, Commodore." John hung up and swung his attention to the rescue efforts. Arnie had it well in hand, but he was the captain of *Nereus*, so this was his problem, too.

**

Pulling the Indian survivors out of the water took an hour, after which *Nereus* retrieved their life raft—John thought the intel weenies might want a look at it—stowed her own boat, and set course for Christmas Island.

Standing watch over the thirty-seven prisoners would stretch *Nereus'* large crew thin for the week's underway, but John had little choice. He couldn't risk allowing the Indians to roam his ship, even if he felt a bit of kindred pity for them. His compassion did extend, however, to meeting with the senior Indian face-to-face.

The captain of INS *Chakra* had not survived, and the navigator, Lieutenant Samantaka Kulkarni, was the senior surviving officer. Two armed masters-at-arms escorted him up to John's cabin three hours after the recovery, and John met him at the door, extending his hand.

"I'm sorry to meet you this way, Lieutenant," he said.

Kulkarni was a slender man, taller than John by at least three or four inches, with jet-black hair and squinting dark eyes. Had he lost glasses in the sinking? John wouldn't ask.

"Thank you for rescuing us, Captain Dalton," Kulkarni said in accented but good English.

"Please, come in." John gestured Kulkarni toward a chair, which the Indian officer took with a tired sigh. "I regret that so few of your crew survived."

Kulkarni nodded tightly. "We were fortunate to get as many off as we did. Your depth charge pattern was well-targeted."

John grimaced, not liking a compliment for the first time in his life. Was he supposed to gloat? Smile? How did someone answer that? Saying *thank you* felt rude. He cleared his throat and poured water for both of them.

"My doctor has seen all your people. I understand there were no major injuries?" he asked instead.

"Yes, thank you." Kulkarni hesitated. "May I ask what our fate will be?"

"We're heading to Christmas Island. You'll fly out of there within a few days, I suppose." John shrugged. "That's not really my department."

"I understand."

"I'm sure you've all been briefed by my XO already, but you'll all be confined to our troop berthing space for now." John was grateful that *Nereus* had space for embarked marines but no marines to sleep in there. It gave him a secure place to put the prisoners, who were far too numerous for his small brig. "Your meals will be delivered there."

"Your first officer made that clear, sir." Kulkarni straightened. "We will not cooperate with questioning, you understand."

"Lieutenant, I'm a submarine captain commanding a tender. I'm not an intelligence officer and would have no idea what to ask even if I wanted to." John shrugged. "I can't make promises for once you reach Christmas Island, but so long as your people abide by the restrictions we've put forth, you'll be treated as guests."

"Guests who are prisoners."

"Lieutenant, I'm not sure what you're hoping for here, but you will do your duty, and I will do mine. We are each officers of navies in conflict," John replied. "I honestly don't know what else you can expect here."

Kulkarni's shoulders slumped. "You are correct, sir. I apologize. I am...I am not accustomed to this."

"Neither am I." John smiled crookedly. "We'll just have to make the best of it. That said, I would like to invite your surviving officers to dinner in the wardroom tonight."

"We'd be honored to accept." Kulkarni hid his grimace well, John thought. He almost managed to look pleased.

***

Dinner was awkward. In hindsight, John wished he hadn't extended the invitation, but he'd felt it was the correct—if old world—thing to do. The six surviving Indian officers had been stiff and uncomfortable, which led to his people acting the same way. It was an experience he didn't care to repeat, so John left the prisoners in troop berthing after that.

He experienced a vague worry or two that Kulkarni might try something stupid, but the young lieutenant kept his mouth shut and his people in line, which was the best John could ask for under the circumstances. Meanwhile, John gritted his teeth, swallowed his pride, and asked Arnie for help with his patrol report.

That turned out to be his second bad idea of the patrol; Arnie's writing skills were worse than his own. Fortunately, Arnie *did* know who was good at writing, and it turned out to be Lieutenant (junior grade) Maeda, who was growing in John's estimation every day. Despite his early uncertainty, Maeda had turned out to be the wardroom's young rockstar, and he was excited for the opportunity to see how a patrol report was written.

Maeda would go far. John made a mental note to ask one of his surface warfare friends, like Nancy Coleman or Jessica Rosario, how to best shepherd the young man's career along. Upon taking command of *Nereus,* John hadn't realized how much about the surface navy he needed to learn...but now he buckled down to figure it all out.

In the interim, however, he had prisoners to deliver to Christmas Island and submarines to repair. Hopefully, his work could save some of his friends from dying. That was about the best he could ask for, wasn't it?

***

Enjoying the story of John Dalton and his comrades in *War of the Submarine*? Continue the series with *I Will Try!* New to the series? Start with *Before the Storm*, available on Amazon and in Kindle Unlimited.

About R.G. Roberts

R.G. Roberts is a veteran of the U.S. Navy, currently living in Connecticut and working as a Manufacturing Manager for a major medical device manufacturer. While an officer in the Navy, R.G. Roberts served on three ships, taught at the Surface Warfare Officer's School, and graduated from the U.S. Naval War College with a masters degree in Strategic Studies & National Security, with a concentration in leadership.

She is a multi-genre author, and has published in military thrillers, science fiction, epic fantasy, and alternate history. She rode horses until she joined the Navy (ships aren't very compatible with high-strung jumpers) and fenced (with swords!) in college. Add in the military experience and history degree, and you get A+ anatomy for a fantasy author. However, since she also enjoyed her time in the Navy and loves history, you'll find her in those genres as well.

You can find R.G. Roberts' website at www.rgrobertswriter.com or find all her links at linktr.ee/rgroberts. From there, you can join her newsletter! Joining the newsletter will get you a free novella or short story, set in either the War of the Submarine or Age of the

Legacy universes (or both, if you like both genres). Newsletters are a twice-a-month affair, so there won't be a ton of spam in your inbox, but you'll be the first to hear about sales, get sneak peeks of new writing, and get to read free short stories from time to time, too!

R.G. Roberts is also one of the authors trying the new-fangled site known as "Ream." It's like Pateron, but made for authors and readers – and especially for superfans! There you will have access to exclusive first looks at all of her works, including early access to chapters of novels, short stories, and more! You can find her Ream at www.ream-stories.com/rgrobertswriter.

Also By the Author

War of the Submarine

Before the Storm
Cardinal Virtues
The War No One Wanted
Fire When Ready
Clean Sweep
I Will Try
Fortune Favors the Bold (Coming Soon!)

War of the Submarine Shorts

Never Take a Recon Marine to a Casino Robbery (subscriber exclusive)
Pedal to the Medal

***

Age the Legacy

Shade
Shadow (Coming Soon!)
Night Rider
Before the Dawn (Coming Soon!)

Legacy Shorts

Prelude to Conquest (subscriber exclusive)
The First Ride (Exclusive on Ream!)
City of Light (Exclusive on Ream!)

***

Alternate History

Against the Wind
Caesar's Command

***

Other Works

Agent of Change (Portal Sci-Fi with an Alternate History Twist)

Fido (Cozy Fantasy Serial, high on humor)

Once Upon a Dragon (Exclusive on Ream!)

Printed in Great Britain
by Amazon

43177164R00056